ROSETTES FOR JI

Jill is afflicted by two unhorsy summer
guests, Melly and Lindo Cortman, and
their prize-winning dogs. Her troubles
increase when they suddenly begin to take
an interest in horses and winning prizes,
and their mother buys them a superb
mare, Blue Shadow, whom Jill would love
to ride. But despite all their
misunderstandings, by the time Chatton
Show comes along, Jill realizes that the
'Cortman kids' are not so bad after all.

About the author:

Ruby Ferguson was born in West Yorkshire and lived in many parts of England and Scotland, travelling extensively in Europe and Canada before her death in the early 1960s.

Her jobs included teaching and political organisation, but her big break in writing came when she started writing detective stories for weekly competitions in the *Manchester Evening News*. Since then 19 of her novels, 7 children's stories and the Jill series have been published.

Ruby Ferguson's interests included dramatics and social work.

Rosettes for Jill

Ruby Ferguson

KNIGHT BOOKS
Hodder and Stoughton

Text copyright © 1957 by Hodder and Stoughton Ltd

First published in 1957 by Hodder and Stoughton Ltd

This edition first published in 1973 by Knight Books

Ninth impression 1983

Set, printed and bound in Great Britain for
Hodder and Stoughton Paperbacks, a
division of Hodder and Stoughton Ltd.,
Mill Road, Dunton Green, Sevenoaks,
Kent (Editorial Office: 47 Bedford
Square, London, WC1 3DP) by
Cox & Wyman Ltd, Reading

ISBN 0 340 17224 X

Contents

1
They're coming!

I HAVE told you a great many episodes from my young and horsewomanly career, but never about the time when the Cortman Kids came to stay with us at the cottage. It happened about two summers ago; and here follows the tale.

In the first place, I had never met the Cortman Kids, and all I knew about them was that their mother had in the Dark Ages of Long Ago been at school with my mother; and I had been instructed to call her Aunt Pamela on the two occasions when she had crossed my path, as it says in sinister stories. She was Mrs Cortman, and Mummy said it was frightfully disrespectful of me to call her daughters the Cortman Kids, especially as one of them was older than I, but it just struck me that way and I went on doing it. Aunt Pamela was apt to rave about them slightly, and by the time that I had learned how beautifully one of them played the piano and how marvellously the other one danced or embroidered or something, I was in a complete state of inferiority complex. Actually Aunt Pamela wasn't bad at all, and always used to crash in at Christmas with quite a decent present, such as a book token, which shows she had the right ideas. I mean, everybody wants a book and knows just what book they want, and who on earth else *can* know? And yet otherwise apparently sane relations keep on sending you *The Third Form at St Helen's* and *Four Girls on Fairy Island* when for weeks you've been flattening your nose against the bookshop window wondering how you can possibly raise one pound twenty-five pence to buy *Practical Show-Jumping*. It really is anguish-making, but Aunt Pamela wasn't like that. Always a book token, so I only had to shout Whoops! and make a bee-line for the bookseller's.

I suppose you have noticed how life's most portentous events hit you right in the eye when you're not expecting it?

We were having breakfast on a perfectly peaceful sunshiny morning, and for once I was lingering over my toast and marmalade because I had done my geometry prep the night before instead of while I was dressing, and I knew where my school hat was, and I had fed the ponies in good time and not at the last minute, so I was feeling frightfully carefree when suddenly Mummy looked up from one of her letters – which the postman had just brought – and said, Oh!

I knew at once it was something a bit shattering, because when it is something nice she says Ah and not Oh; but even I with my talent for expecting the worst from all grown-ups' letters didn't guess *how* shattering.

'What's the matter?' I said. 'Have they let you down again about the colour of the new curtains?'

'Let me down?' Mummy said briskly. 'Of course not. It's from Aunt Pamela. We'll have to do some thinking.'

'Is she coming to stay?' I said; and Mummy said, on the contrary Aunt Pamela was taking her husband to Majorca for two months to recuperate after an operation and wondered if Mummy could find somewhere in our district for the two girls to stay where they would be under Mummy's eye. Aunt Pamela thought that a spell of country life would be good for them, and was sure that Mummy would know of some simple, homely family who would take them for a few weeks and let them live a simple homely life.

'What about Moss Farm?' I said. 'Mrs Overdale is frightfully simple and homely and she has eight or nine children, so two Cortman Kids wouldn't make a lot of difference.'

'There's no question of it,' said Mummy, in her most determined voice, and my spirits flopped into my sandals and ran out through the toes because I knew what was coming — 'Of course the girls must come here.'

'Why?' I said miserably, and Mummy said, 'Because we'd love to have them.'

I put down my last corner of toast. 'Oh, help!' I said. 'That ruins everything.'

'Ruins what?' said Mummy.

'Well Ann and Diana and I have got everything planned for the holidays. We're going to do a lot of intensive equitation in the evenings from now till the shows begin, and we're certainly not going to have any time for strangers.'

Mummy said she thought my attitude was disgusting, and reminded her of the old saying, 'Here comes a stranger, let's throw a brick at him,' and that was what was the matter with the world today and started wars; and I said I hadn't a single thing against strangers in general, but I couldn't think of anything worse than to spend the next three precious months trailing the Cortman Kids round Chatton, because from my point of view they were a dead loss as they didn't ride, and would, therefore, be completely incompatible, and why on earth couldn't Aunt Pamela send her beastly daughters to some people who liked doing the things *they* liked doing?

'Blow!' I said. 'It's just the end.'

I could see already that it wasn't any use and the worst was going to happen. When I got home from school at teatime Mummy had already written to Aunt Pamela to tell her the girls were to come and stay with us.

'And I suppose they're to have my room,' I said bitterly.
'That's O.K., a bit more torture's neither here nor there.'

'Oh, buck up, Jill,' said Mummy, laughing. 'They're going
to have a room at Mrs Mills', it's only twenty yards along
the lane, so that's one thing you needn't suffer over. I've
arranged it all.'

For the next three days I kept hoping (a) that it was a
dream and I should suddenly wake up and find it wasn't
true, or (b) that something would happen to make the Cortman Kids want to go somewhere else, because I couldn't for
the life of me see what attraction there could be for them
at Chatton where, if you don't ride, you might as well be
dead.

My friend Ann Derry said, 'Perhaps they won't be so
bad as you think!'

'They will,' I said. 'I can feel it coming, like a Thing from
Space.'

'Well, they needn't interfere with us,' she said, cheerfully.
'I mean, for the first day or two you'll probably have to drag
them round and show them where the tennis courts are and
where the park is, and where they can get their beastly hair
cut; and after that they'll go their own simple, homely way
and we can forget them, and get on with the ponies, and I
did the most beautiful, beautiful collected trot I've ever done
in my life this morning, and I'm dying to show you – if I
can do it again.'

I said, I hoped she was right about the Cortmans, and we
went on up to the Riding School, and Ann did her collected
trot to show me and Mrs Darcy, and I told Mrs Darcy all
my woes. She merely laughed and said, 'You'll just have to
make horsewomen out of them, Jill, I wouldn't put it past
you,' and I said darkly that there were some things that
nobody could make out of anything.

The next morning brought a letter from the Cortman girls themselves, thanking Mummy for her invitation and saying how thrilled they were to be coming to stay with us in the country, because actually they lived at Cheltenham which was very towny nowadays.

They signed the letter, Melly and Lindo Cortman, and I said, 'What names! More like spaniels.' Mummy said, 'It's funny you should say that, because just over the page there's a P.S. and it says, "What dogs do you keep?" What do you think that means?'

'I know only too well what it means,' I said. 'There are two kinds of people in the world, horsy people and doggy people, and I'm the horsy kind and they're doggy. That's what it means.'

'But you're very fond of dogs,' said Mummy.

'Yes, I know I am, but I don't keep dogs because I don't think it would be fair to them when I give all my time to the ponies. I mean, if you go in for any kind of animals you've got to make them feel they're the most important things on earth to you, and when horses are most important things in the world to you you can't convince dogs that they are.'

Mummy said that would be enough, and she got my general meaning and didn't want me to tie myself in knots.

'Possibly Mello and Lindy, or whatever they're called, are bringing a couple of champion Alsatians with them.' I couldn't resist flinging this out, and then we both began to giggle, though Mummy looked a bit shaken.

I said, ought we to send a postcard to say we hadn't any dogs? Mummy said that as they seemed to think the matter urgent enough for a letter, we had better send a telegram in return, so we went to the village post office and did so. To economise on words – which one instinctively does in these expensive days – I wrote on the form, No Dogs Here and handed it in over the counter to Mrs Anderson's daughter, whose eyebrows shot up practically into her hair as she began to count, and following her astonished gaze I observed already in the post office two corgis, three Pekes, a Labrador and a bull terrier. Miss Anderson obviously thought me completely mad, but then so do most people.

By now I felt I needed some sympathy, so I went round to Ann's again. She met me at the door, and told me that George, her pony, was awful. I asked, why awful? and she said he had got so clever he could undo a halter with his front teeth. I was interested and asked if I might see this done, so we went out and got George and put a halter on him and tied him to the gate-post of the little paddock behind the Derry's house. He stood looking at us in a dim sort of way, and Ann said, 'We'd better go out of sight, he won't do it while we're watching.' So we went into the house and watched him behind the curtains, but he just stood there in a trance, occasionally tossing his head and blowing gently as he watched the sparrows picking grains of corn round his feet.

'He isn't going to do it,' said Ann. 'He isn't even trying.'

'Perhaps you dreamt it,' I said, and she said that on the contrary George had spent practically half the previous day undoing halters with his front teeth. I started to tell her about the Cortmans and the dog-telegram, and we forgot George, and just as I finished the story we looked round and there was George, half-way down the paddock, with his eyes fixed on space and his feet hidden in daisies, and the halter hanging by its end to the gate-post.

'There you are!' said Ann. 'He's done it, the minute we turned our backs.'

'Well, let's make him do it again,' I said. 'Perhaps Pam untied him.'

Not to go into sordid details, we spent the afternoon watching George untying his halter with his front teeth – which he soon began to do obligingly under our very eyes – and I could not help thinking sadly how this and other simple horsy pleasures might soon be snatched from me by the obligations of hospitality to the unwanted Cortman Kids.

On Friday afternoon I had just got back from school and was happily planning what I should do when Mummy said, 'It's time you changed, Jill, to come to the station.'

'Oh, help!' I said, for I had momentarily forgotten that the awful moment had arrived. 'I don't see why I need go. Actually, I've got to take Rapide to the farrier, he's cast another nail.'

But I could see I wasn't going to get out of it, so I dragged myself wearily upstairs and joylessly began to take off my gym tunic and climb into my grey coat and skirt instead of my jodhs and old blue shirt for which my soul was yearning.

2
They've come

MELLY and Lindo got off the train. It had to be Melly and Lindo because they were the only two people of the right ages. They had on tweed skirts and windbreakers, and one of them had a fair plait and the other a ginger one.

Mummy said, 'There they are,' and sped away towards them, while I followed a lot more slowly because I didn't see why I should give them the impression that I was dying to meet them. By the time I got up to them the fair-plaited one was saying, 'The dogs are in the van.'

'There you are, Mummy,' I said. 'Alsatians.'

'Actually, they're not,' said the fair-plaited one. 'There's a Corgi and a West Highland terrier.'

'This is Jill,' said Mummy unnecessarily.

'I'm Melly,' said the fair plait, 'and this is my sister Lindo.'

'Hullo,' I said. 'You're lucky to break up so soon. We don't break up for another week.'

'Neither do we, actually,' said Lindo. 'But we had to miss the last week of the term to come here.'

I felt like saying, what a pity, but before I had time to decide whether to make this slightly sarky observation the two girls and Mummy were on their way to the luggage van to sort out the dogs. These proved to be quite nice dogs, and very well kept and well behaved, so I really hadn't a thing to complain of, which was a bit galling.

We all got into a taxi, rattled through the town, swished along the country lanes and eventually arrived at the cottage.

Melly and Lindo thought it was marvellous and only wished it was a bit bigger so that there would be room for them to sleep – instead of at Mrs Mills' up the lane – but of course if it were any larger that would spoil its old-world charm; and I could see Mummy being more and more impressed by their intelligence, and thought, This is going to be awful for me to live up to!

We had tea in the sitting-room, and the two dogs lay on the rug like images and didn't ask for cake. I felt a bit sorry for them, being as well-trained as that, and remembering my friend Diana Bush's cheerful cairns who climb all over you to get at the fairy buns the minute tea appears. I wondered what would happen if I offered the Cortman dogs a bit of fruit cake. However, tea was over, and Mummy said she would go round with the girls to see their room at Mrs Mills', and they would soon be back and then I could show them the garden.

The minute they were gone I rushed upstairs and put on my old shirt and jodhs. It was heaven. Then I went down and through the orchard to the gate of my small paddock and my ponies came trotting to me with expectant eyes and pricked ears, wondering why I was so late.

'You may well wonder!' I said dismally, and gave them their sugar. 'You – ' I added, to Rapide, 'are supposed to go to the farrier's, and I was going to ride Black Boy and lead you, and it would have been fun, but I daren't go now because it will look as if I'm dodging the Cortmans, and Mummy will be furious. Life is hard.'

I leaned on the gate, and the ponies nuzzled my hands with their soft noses. They couldn't understand why I didn't take them out. Then I heard voices.

'There's Jill,' I heard Mummy say. 'She's dying to show you her ponies.'

Actually, I wasn't doing anything of the kind, but I didn't want to appear mean, so I turned round and said, 'Oh, hullo.'

'I say!' said Lindo. 'Are those your ponies? They do look nice.'

I knew at once that this girl was completely unhorsy, as the ponies didn't look nice at all. Black Boy had been rolling and was very muddy, and Rapide kept pecking with his off hind foot, the one that needed the farrier, and any horsy person would have said at once, That one seems to have lost a nail.

'Actually, they look a bit slummy at the moment,' I said.

'I suppose they make a lot of work,' said Lindo politely. 'I mean, it's bad enough grooming dogs.'

I could tell she was just trying to show an interest, and preferred Melly who said right out, 'We don't know anything about ponies. I suppose you go for rides on them. But you can't ride two at once, so why do you have two?'

I explained patiently that my main interest in life was showing my ponies in competitive events, that fortunately for me I had the kind of friends who did the same, that show-jumping was the most fascinating occupation on earth, and that if you had two ponies you would not be let down by a strained fetlock or minor ailment on the day. Also, it was more interesting to jump two ponies than one since each had his own individual style.

'It sounds fascinating,' said Lindo, looking quite blank, and Melly said, 'Jolly complicated, I should think.'

'Well, there's a small Show next week,' I said, 'so you'll be able to see.'

Lindo said, 'Good,' in an absent-minded kind of way; and Melly said, 'You don't have to bother about entertaining us. Mummy said, we weren't to get in your way. We like going for long walks with the dogs.'

'That's okay,' I said; but I didn't see how they could help getting in my way in a cottage the size of ours; and for once in my life I found myself wishing with all my heart that I dwelt in one of the stately homes of England with ninety-five rooms and miles of grounds extending in all directions, so that one need practically never see one's guests if one didn't want to, especially if their interests were not compatible with one's own.

'If you'll excuse me,' I said, 'I think I'll take Rapide down to the farrier tonight, or he'll have that shoe off.'

'Gosh, what a bind,' said Melly.

I said rather unconvincingly that nothing to do with the ponies was a bind, and Lindo said that was just how she felt about the dogs, and an uneasy silence fell.

Twenty-four hours later, Ann and her young sister Pam and I were trotting happily over the Common, I on Rapide, Pam riding Black Boy for me, and Ann on George.

'Well, what are they like?' said Ann.

'Not too bad really,' I said. 'Mummy made me walk them miles through the woods this afternoon with the dogs, but once I've shown them where the walks are I should think they won't be any more bother. They like going for walks, and they do embroidery, and play tennis, which I think is frightfully worthy but uninspiring. Mummy says we'll have to take them with us to the gymkhana at Queen's Tracey next Saturday.'

'That won't kill us,' said Ann, 'and it may be an eye-opener for them. There's to be a dressage exhibition by Colonel Somebody, I'm looking forward to that.'

'Me too,' I said. 'Come on, let's gallop. I've got to let off steam.'

With the wind rushing through my hair I forgot my woes.

Meanwhile, Melly and Lindo arranged to sleep their dogs at the kennels, and have them out in the daytime, which they spent at our house; though considering that they were taken for a long walk in the morning and a long walk in the evening, and slept all the afternoon, I must say we hardly noticed them. As a matter of fact, I was really sorry for the poor things, they were so well behaved; and when they lay on the rug they were so neatly placed, nose by nose and tail by tail, not all in a happy huddle mixed up with cushions and cardigans, like Diana Bush's cairns.

I must say, Melly and Lindo tried to show a polite interest in the ponies, though their ignorance was appalling. But what was worst was the way they talked about all the things they had done, and all the places they had been to, and all the games they had played with frightful success – not boastingly but just as matter of course – until I felt about five years old and not quite right in the head. I began banging books about, and left my room in an awful litter, and put my fawn shirt on with such fury that three buttons popped off, shot across the floor, and disappeared under the furniture.

I started muttering appropriate oaths, and Mummy said, 'Really, Jill. If you'd only do things more quietly – and if you'd sewed those buttons on when they needed it they wouldn't have been all over the floor now. Just find them without upsetting the whole house.'

'One's broken,' I said angrily.

'There may be another in my work-box.'

I found a needle and some fawn thread, and said, 'If

Melly and Lindo start telling me again about when they both won prizes in the tennis tournament at Bournemouth I shall go raving mad. And they can both dive from the top board but one, and they've flown to Dublin and back, and if they're frightfully good while their father and mother are away they're going to get taken to Switzerland next year. All I can say is, thank goodness it's the Queen's Tracey gymkhana on Saturday. I'll be able to show them something they can't do. I'm sure to win a showing class with Black Boy, and I ought to be in the first three in the fourteen-and-under jumping, and I've entered for the senior too, with Rapide, and some of the competitions are just a gift for him. I'm not usually a pot-hunter, but I hope I come back plastered with rosettes on Saturday.'

'Oh, dear,' said Mummy, laughing. 'Is it as bad as that? Well, I hope for your sake you show them a thing or two on Saturday.'

3

No good at Queen's Tracey

MELLY and Lindo, believe it or not, had never been to a gymkhana.

'Crumbs!' I said. 'You're only half-educated.'

I was glad we were going to Queen's Tracey, because it was always a very good affair. It was an old, dilapidated house with lovely grounds, which belonged to some nice, horsy people called Fletcher who farmed and rode and trained young hunters. Every year they laid on this event in aid of local charities, and it was very good fun, and I thought just the thing to impress anybody who hadn't been to a gymkhana before.

I was simply praying for a fine day, so much so that I couldn't sleep the night before and kept on getting out of bed to peer at the sky and see what the clouds looked like. Every time the moon was clear I was pleased, and then a bit later it would be clouded over and my spirits would go flopping down like dying goldfish. I got up about seven and it was rather grey, but I told myself that all the best days start like that.

Ann came round before nine, with George, because we always do our grooming together before an event.

'What's it going to be like?' I said, blinking nervously up at the sky.

'All right, I should think,' she said. 'Why?'

'Because I don't want to ride in a mac,' I said. 'I want

everything to be absolutely It today, because of showing-off to Melly and Lindo.'

'You're a goon,' she said.

'It's all right for you,' I said. 'You don't have to more-or-less live with them and hear about all the marvellous things they can do.'

'Well, they can't ride,' Ann said, 'and you can, so that's one way of getting them out of your hair.'

'Strangely enough,' I said, sarkily, 'that was my idea.'

She then threw a stable rubber at me, and I sloshed the saddle soap at her, and the next minute we were haring round the orchard with the ponies after us; and into this bedlam walked Melly and Lindo and said in a very superior way, 'What on earth are you doing?'

'Loosening up the ponies,' said Ann, who was quicker than I was at thinking of the right thing to say. 'Come on, Jill, let's catch them and get cracking.'

We started the grooming, both working on the same pony together. There were three to do, so it took quite a long time, especially as I was particularly fussy that day and had actually gone to the frightful expense of blueing ten pence on a Gleemo shampoo from Woolworth for the tails.

Melly and Lindo stood watching all the time, and I really wished they wouldn't because it made me nervous. They also kept asking why, why, why, which was a bit putting-off. Then Ann went into the house and collected thread, scissors, and needles for the manes, and we started plaiting. This is something one literally cannot do when watched, and I made an awful mess of Black Boy and had to pull it out and start again and felt an awful fool, and I could have murdered Lindo when she began to giggle and said, 'Do you comb it out and set it?'

'Gosh!' muttered Ann through her teeth. 'I'll comb *you* out, any minute now.'

We put on the final polish till our arms ached, but in the end the three of them stood looking absolutely beautiful, Black Boy like shining jet, and Rapide like dark mahogany and George like lighter mahogany, their hoofs oiled and speckless, and their eyes bright with excitement as they gently swished their silken tails.

'I'm tying this halter very tight, double knots for you, George my boy,' said Ann. 'No sitting down in the dust.'

'What happens now?' said Melly.

'We go and get changed ourselves, and then a quick lunch. We've got to leave here at one.'

'How do you get there?' said Lindo.

'Helicopter,' I said sarkily. 'And some friends are calling for Mummy and you in their car.'

Ann and I went up to my room to dress. For once in my life I had assembled everything ready, instead of having the mad last-minute search for the right tie.

'Fawn shirt, yellow tie, and my best jodhs,' I said to Ann. 'I suppose we'll have to wear our jackets to go in, but I'd like to ride without. Are we taking our blacks in case we have to go up for any Cups?'

She said she hadn't brought hers, because actually it was an informal affair and she didn't think anybody would; and anyway, she thought that Melly and Lindo would be sufficiently impressed by seeing all my rosettes and I could keep back my black coat for another occasion as a sort of *pièce de résistance*.

We preened ourselves in front of the glass in my room until there wasn't a hair out of place, and put on just enough lipstick to look interesting, because in those days when I was only fourteen, Mummy was down on me like a ton of bricks if I tried to look sophisticated. Then we had an earnest discussion about whether hard hats or crash caps. Believe me, we didn't go on like this as a rule before a gymkhana; it was all in aid of Melly and Lindo. In the end we decided on our caps, and bolted downstairs.

'Are you taking macs?' said Mummy. 'It's looking a bit doubtful.'

'No,' I said firmly, realizing that Melly and Lindo – who had on skirts and blouses and school blazers – were looking at my get-up with furtive respect and admiration.

Mrs Crosby, our daily help, brought in plates of jolly-looking sandwiches; cakes, fruit, lemonade and coffee.

'Are you feeling quite well?' she said to me. 'Because you're usually tearing my kitchen apart looking for your hat, and messing boot polish about while I'm trying to butter the bread.'

'I prepared everything last night,' I said, looking dignified.

She said, 'Well, that's something new,' and I said, 'We live and learn,' and she said, 'If you've found that out it's a step in the right direction, or is it?'

Ann and I saddled and bridled the ponies, and set off quietly. We had less than two miles to go. The sun had not managed to come out, and the sky was grey, but when we got to Queen's Tracey the field looked beautiful, surrounded by fine trees, and it was exciting to see the show ring and lots of spectators already milling about, and people we knew arriving with their ponies all the time.

We tied up the ponies and went to fetch our numbers. I felt much more worked up than usual, and hated the hanging around which doesn't worry me as a rule. Then our party arrived, and everybody wished us good luck.

'Just look at that girl,' said Melly, 'Isn't she marvellous?'

The girl was Susan Pyke, of whom you must know if you have read my previous books, and as usual she was prancing around on a rather wicked-looking pony, reined in too tight. She gave me a very friendly wave, and the pony did a sort of polka.

'She's in the Lower Fifth,' said Ann. 'She's one of the world's horrors, and if she doesn't jump a clear round she argues with the judge.'

Then we were called in for the first showing class. There was a big entry, and to my dismay from the very first moment I felt things weren't going quite right. Black Boy took a dislike to the pony in front – which was a hogged cob ridden by a farmer's son called Phil Loseby who was never very nice to other people's ponies – and he hung back and was crowded by the pony behind, which upset him.

We cantered a bit, and were called in fifth, and there to my humiliation we stayed. Ann was third, and when she came out with her yellow rosette, I said, 'What on earth happened to me?'

'I don't know,' she said. 'But when you went round the corners, Black Boy had his head bent the wrong way.'

This put me off so much that from that moment I had a helpless feeling that I was going to do nothing right, and you know how fatal that is in any kind of sport. I collected a third with Rapide in the second showing class because the judge said he was the cleanest pony; and then it began to rain, just in time for the first jumping class. Ann jumped early and got six faults, and when she came out, George was walking on three legs and winced when Ann felt his off fore, so he was out of action from then on. I rode fourteenth and it was very slippery and I got twelve faults. Nobody did very well, in fact, there wasn't a single clear round; but three people got two faults and jumped it off, and that was that.

Then there was a game for the under-twelves, and Mummy came across to me with Melly and Lindo.

'You got a yellow rosette, didn't you?' said Melly as though to encourage the infant.

I would have liked to gnash my teeth, like they do in books, but I don't know how you do it. Mummy was just beginning to say that I really ought to have brought my mac when it stopped raining and the sun burst forth strongly.

Ann and I went off and soothed our tortured feelings by eating three ice creams each.

'The sun's blazing now,' she said, 'and the ground is only wet on the surface. You'll probably do awfully well in the under-sixteen jumping.'

'Gosh, it isn't my day,' I said. 'I'm doomed.'

There were some competitions next, and I insisted on Ann riding Black Boy for the Musical Mats. To make a long, sad story shorter I didn't seem to be able to concentrate and was out the second time, and Ann won it. I won my heat on Rapide in the Bending, but by some frightful mischance he missed out a pole in the final and we were fourth, and there were only two prizes.

I rested him nicely during the Handy Hunter, and had a cup of tea myself; and by then the ground had dried out and looked lovely, and there was nothing to hinder me making a good show in the under-sixteen jumping except my jinx or gremlin or whatever it was that was biting me. One thing that put me off was that Susan Pyke jumped just before me, and I was quite sure that her wicked-looking pony would have several refusals and then bolt out of the ring, instead of which he jumped as though inspired and she got a clear round. This shook me considerably, and my nervousness transferred itself to my pony, which is inexcusable in a rider. My timing was bad, and I had only myself to blame that I finally rode out with six faults, which put me out of the running.

'You are having bad luck,' Mummy said.

'Oh, it's just not my day,' I said, turning away to hide my disappointment. I very rarely feel like crying, but I did then, and I was furious and ashamed, and horrified with dread that I might actually weep. I had to hide my feelings and watch the rest of the jumping, because after all one cannot look unsporting; and then came the Open Jumping, and an exhibition of dressage by this Colonel Somebody, and it was all over.

Ann and I jogged ungracefully homewards.

'At least,' she said, 'we didn't have the bother of bringing our black coats to collect those cups.'

'One yellow rosette!' I said, bitterly. 'And fifty pence.'

'Speak for yourself!' said my friend. 'It seems to have slipped your supersonic memory that I collected third place in the showing class that you were *fifth* in. *And* I won the Musical Mats – a dandy brush and a tin of saddle soap.'

'We're coming on,' I said, bitterly. 'One of these days we'll win a potato race!'

'It's frightfully tough on you,' said Ann. 'Just when you wanted to impress Melly and Lindo. And to think that a fortnight ago you won a Cup and two firsts at Limwell Manor. Gosh, that's life!'

I got home and spent ages rubbing down the ponies and giving them their feeds. Then, because I was afraid they might be feeling a bit blue too, I put an arm round each of them and said, 'It wasn't a bit your faults, it was all mine. I rode badly, and I apologize to both of you.'

I thought that Melly and Lindo would have been bored by the gymkhana and that we shouldn't hear any more of it, but all through supper and for the rest of the evening they could talk about nothing else. They took it for granted that I wasn't much good, but raved on and on about the Open Jumping. Could anybody do it? How soon did one learn to do it? It looked so easy. And that man who made the horse walk backwards and sideways. It looked frightfully simple and rather silly, and they didn't see the point. Anybody could make a horse walk backwards, their coal-man did, you only had to push it and say Grrrr.

I patiently told them that dressage was an advanced form of equitation, being the complete control of a trained horse, but they still didn't see it.

In the end, Mummy came to my aid and suggested to Melly and Lindo, wasn't it time they took the dogs for a run, they must be bored after being left alone all afternoon, and they fell for this, and I got a bit of peace.

4
Less good when showing off

WHEN I woke on Monday morning I felt happier. It was a lovely bright morning, and the holidays had begun, and I told myself I just could not care less if the Cortmans despised me. I had plenty of my own friends, and who were the Cortmans anyway? Just ignoramuses.

It was about seven o'clock, so I flew out of bed and put on my shabby old jodhs that I love, and a sloppy sweater, and my old gym shoes that have gone at the seams and oozed down the silent stairs to the kitchen where I put the kettle on for a cup of tea. When the tea was made I poured Mummy's into her pink cup and carried it up.

'Oh, Jill, you angel,' she said. 'I was just dying for one. And it always seems to be when I'm dying for a cup that you sleep late.'

I drank two cups myself, and rushed out to feed the ponies and put them in the orchard. They were full of joy, and their big dark eyes sparkled when they saw the sunny morning and smelt the orchard grass, and off they went in an excited canter, tossing their manes and giving each other little friendly pecks and butts.

I sat on the gate and watched them until I smelt the bacon frying, and then I went in, starving.

'Oh, isn't it lovely and peaceful,' I broke out. 'Why on

earth can't Melly and Lindo go out for the day by themselves?'

Mummy didn't say anything, but she looked worried, and I felt I had been rather mean and silly, so to make up for this I offered to go and feed the hens. After I had done this, I unfortunately didn't fasten the door of the hen house properly, and as our hens are frightfully tame and a bit too friendly they followed me back and came streaming into the cottage.

'Oh, help!' cried Mummy, trying to collect them, and calling them by name; but Ernestine, Petunia, Alicia, Marguerite, Dorinda, and Wilhelmine were having much too good a time, and into this bedlam walked Melly and Lindo, looking as if they thought we'd gone mad.

I simply hated them, and said coldly, 'You'd better go into the sitting-room, the hens seem to have got in here.' Mummy was by now laughing so much that I couldn't do anything but join in, and we giggled crazily. Then Mrs Crosby arrived and of course she had the hens collected and disposed of in about two minutes. The master's touch.

'What are you girls going to do this morning?' said Mummy as we joined the Cortmans in the sitting-room.

'I've got a riding lesson at nine,' I said, thankfully.

'Oh, I see, you're just having lessons,' said Melly, as though that explained everything.

I felt like pointing out to her that, in riding, just as in any other sport such as golf or tennis or skating, you went on having lessons for ever and ever, unless you were one of those conceited people who thought they were wonderful and didn't need lessons, in which case you soon found out you were wrong; but I simply couldn't be bothered to waste so much breath, so I let the implied insult stand.

'Where do you go?' said Lindo.

'To the riding school,' I said shortly.

'Oh, can we come and watch?' said Lindo.

Oh, help, no! I thought, but to my horror, Mummy said, 'Yes, of course you can. Take them along, Jill, it'll be interesting for them.'

Melly said that they had to go and collect their dogs first from the Kennels, but would follow on later if Mummy would tell them the way.

With my doom hanging round my neck, so to speak, I went and mounted Rapide and rode to Mrs Darcy's.

I found her drinking a cup of tea in the little paddock, and watching Pansy who was lunging a grey pony which laid its ears back, tried to bite the rope, kicked, and dug its toes in.

'Look at that!' said Mrs Darcy, waving her cup of tea towards the pony and losing half of it. 'A good pony absolutely ruined because the woman who owns her hasn't the slightest idea how to train a pony and won't be told. This one has been allowed to develop every known fault, and now she's completely out of hand she's brought to me and I'm told to make a good pony out of her. What can one do? Not much. And then the owner takes her away and isn't satisfied, and tells everybody that Mrs Darcy's no good with horses. People who don't understand how to control animals oughtn't to be allowed to own them – and I mean proper, intelligent control, not letting the poor thing get right out of hand and then whipping her for bad behaviour.'

'She's a nice-looking pony,' I said, 'and she's got a good head.'

'Oh, she's nice enough if you put her in a field and give her sugar and let her have all her own way. But she bolts, and she bites other horses, and she's a menace on the road, and she's two years old and it's too late. The owner will finally sell her, and she'll be whacked into submission and her spirit broken, and it makes my blood boil. If people don't know how to train animals kindly and firmly they oughtn't to – oh, I said that before. Pardon my bad temper. Jill, would you like to go and catch the riding school ponies, as Pansy has her hands full at present, because when she's finished she's going to take a party of beginners on the Common.'

'Right-ho,' I said. 'I don't mind if I stay and help all morning. I've nothing else to do.'

'I thought you had some visitors staying with you?'

'Hmph!' I snorted.

I started sorting out some halters, and Mrs Darcy said, 'I hear you had an off-day at Queen's Tracey on Saturday.'

'Off-day!' I said. 'I was ghastly.'

'Well, that's nothing. Everybody has them.'

I said bitterly that nobody at Queen's Tracey had shown any sign of having an off-day but me, and I knew very well it was my own fault because I'd wanted to show off and had pressed the ponies and upset them; and she said, why on earth should I of all people want to show off? And I said, to impress those horrible Cortmans, who now thought I was just a beginner, and they were coming up this morning to see me have a lesson and I couldn't think of anything worse.

'Oh, you are mad, Jill,' said Mrs Darcy. 'You know I haven't got an animal here that you can't ride. If you want to impress them you can get up on Barometer if you care to.'

Considering that Barometer stood seventeen hands, and had a mouth like reinforced concrete – possibly owing to the fact that he belonged to a man called Mr Peachmonger who looked as if he were entirely *made* of reinforced concrete – I said thank you very much, I'd rather not look like a sparrow sitting on the Rock of Gibraltar, Cortmans or no Cortmans, and we both laughed and I felt better.

'I'm awfully silly to care,' I said. 'They've never seen ponies before, and don't know the first thing about riding, and they ask idiotic questions, and I don't know why on earth I should let people like that get me down.'

The riding school ponies were grazing peacefully in their field, and offered no resistance when I went round, patting each one in turn and putting on the halters. There were seven of them: Monty, Chevalier, Princess, Fanciful, Grandeur, Rosetta, and Seascape.

'I'll get them ready,' I shouted to Pansy as I led the bunch in.

Soon they were all ready and the children arrived, three of them with their own ponies. Pansy, who had been having a little more success with the bad pony, patted her and put her away; then she rushed off to tidy herself, and soon the whole party set off along the grass verge of the road towards the Common, laughing and chattering.

Mrs Darcy came down and said we might as well start my lesson, and just as I was hoping that Melly and Lindo had changed their minds and found something better to do, they turned up.

'Oh, is this where you learn to ride?' said Lindo, looking round in a disappointed way. 'I thought there would have been dozens of horses and riders prancing about and jumping over walls.'

'You ought to go to the circus,' I said in disgust.

'Lindo evidently doesn't know anything about riding schools,' said Mrs Darcy sweetly. 'But then none of us can know all about everything, can we? Let's get on with your lesson, Jill. I'm afraid these two will be frightfully bored and not see the point of a collected walk at all, but I do assure them there's more in it than meets the eye, and I haven't time to go into details about the technicalities of riding to people who aren't interested, anyway.'

Melly and Lindo were not only impressed by this, but also effectively shut up, while I found myself feeling as cool as a cucumber. Mrs Darcy put me through it, doing everything again and again.

'There!' she said at last. 'What's to stop you doing it like that in the show ring?'

'Only Fate,' I said darkly.

Melly and Lindo didn't say anything about being bored, but to my surprise asked if they might have a look round the place before we left. I suppose it was their burning thirst for any kind of information. So first of all I took them into the tack room, and for their own good showed them the photographs on the walls of Mrs Darcy being presented with lavish Cups by all sorts of important people, and Mrs Darcy jumping at Harringay and Richmond, and being shaken hands with by the Duke of Gloucester; and for the first time they really did seem impressed by these visible signs of success, though they had simply never heard of the leading people in the world of equitation and thought the British Show Jumping team was something to do with hurdling!

Then Pansy came back with the children, who all jumped down and skilfully unsaddled the ponies and rushed vigorously into the tack room and began to clean their own tack, whistling and singing.

'Good gracious!' said Melly in horror. 'Don't they have a man to do that?'

Pansy looked at her scornfully and said, 'It's part of the training. At this riding school we train people to be able to do everything, not just throw the reins to other people when they've had their ride. We don't consider people who do that have any right to call themselves horsewomen. All these children think it's part of the fun to feed and groom ponies, and clean tack and muck out stables, and that's the right spirit.'

Melly didn't look very convinced. Meanwhile, Pansy led out the enormous Barometer – who was being looked after during his owner's absence – and prepared him for his morning exercise.

Lindo looked on approvingly and said, 'If I rode, that's the sort of horse I'd want to ride.'

'You'd look like a sparrow sitting on the Rock of Gibraltar,' I said.

'No, I shouldn't. I've got long legs.'

'Well, you'd look like a daddy-long-legs sitting on a grand piano,' said Melly, which was the first intelligent remark I had ever heard her make, so I laughed encouragingly. This must have encouraged her too much, as she began to ask Mrs Darcy a lot of silly questions, and I felt so ashamed that I fairly dragged her away, and we went home. When we got home Melly and Lindo said, goodness, they hadn't taken the dogs out yet and must do so at once, and I heaved a sigh of relief. I felt that I couldn't bear anybody's company any longer except my own and that of a pony, so I turned Rapide into the orchard and saddled Black Boy and went for a ride.

We crossed the Common and rode into the beechwoods. It was beautifully silent, like in a Cathedral, with only now and then the cheep of a bird or the rustle of some little creature in the undergrowth, and Black Boy's hoofs made hardly a sound on the thick carpet of leaf mould laid down over hundreds of years. It was absolute bliss to be riding like this, far from Melly and Lindo and their silly questions and superior remarks, and I wished it could go on for ever. There were hundreds of broad tracks to explore, and we cantered along over the soft ground while Black Boy enjoyed himself, and shook his mane and pretended to see fairies, which he sometimes does, because he has quite a lot of imagination.

Unfortunately, I quite forgot the time and then found my watch had stopped because I had forgotten to wind it up, so when I got home for lunch everybody else had half finished and Mummy was annoyed, so once more I looked small before the people I wanted to impress. I felt it was very hard luck.

While we were washing up after lunch – and I must say, Melly and Lindo were very decent about helping with such jobs, which pleased Mummy – it began to rain, so there was nothing for it but to read most of the afternoon. I rushed upstairs and got *Practical Show-Jumping*. Melly and Lindo said, could I lend them something, and I said in a rather high-hat way that all my books were about horses and I didn't think they'd care for them, but probably they'd like something out of Mummy's room. So they went and rummaged on Mummy's shelves, and Melly got *War and Peace* and said she might as well start it though she hadn't a hope of finishing it. Lindo couldn't find anything she liked – which I thought was extremely unintelligent of her – and finally decided to do a jigsaw.

We went into the sitting-room and sprawled in chairs, and Melly and I began to read, but she proved to be one of those people who can't read without muttering, so I started to read aloud to make her shut up, and she said, 'What's the matter with you?' And I said, 'I wish you wouldn't mutter, I've just got to a very technical bit,' and she said, 'Oh, you and your stupid horses! You can't really like a book like that, you're only trying to show off; all beginners do.'

I started yelling at her, and the next minute we were having a flaming row. Lindo went on calmly doing her jigsaw, until I accidentally grabbed hold of the table cloth and the next minute the jigsaw was all over the floor, and Lindo gave a shriek of fury. Mummy, who was trying to work in her bedroom, came rushing down, and I was for it. She took me upstairs and gave me a lecture and said she had never seen such ridiculous behaviour as mine, it was quite uncivilized not to be able to be polite and hospitable to one's guests, and she didn't know what had come over me; and I tried to explain what an awful effect Melly and Lindo had on me, but it sounded very thin even to me. Mummy said gravely that if being keen on horses was going to make me so one-sided and narrow-minded that I couldn't show tolerance for people who were not horsy, then she'd have to think seriously whether it wouldn't be a good thing to send me to a boarding school where they didn't ride, before I got my disposition ruined and became a sort of pony-maniac, because she didn't want to have that kind of daughter.

I was horrified and said, 'Oh, Mummy, don't. I swear I'll be tolerant to Melly and Lindo, and I'm not a maniac about ponies at all; but they're so *smug* and they think I'm no good.'

Mummy said, 'Cheer up, everything's going to be all right. Now let's go down and make some dripping toast for tea.'

After tea Ann rang up and asked me to go round; and I found out afterwards that while I was away Mummy had opened the cupboard where my Cups are kept, and the drawer full of rosettes, and had shown them to Melly and Lindo, a thing that I would have died rather than do; but it was decent of Mummy to give me a boost and try to restore my self-respect.

5
Prize dogs

WHEN my friends came round we talked ponies all the
time, and Melly and Lindo looked at us in a dim sort of
way as if we were not quite all there. After Mummy's
lecture I did try hard to find a sort of common meeting
ground with them, but it was nearly hopeless. We just
didn't mix, and yet in our small cottage we were thrown
together so much — except when I escaped for rides or
lessons — and I found myself longing more and more for that
ancestral mansion with thousands of rooms and miles of
grounds.

Then one evening Melly was reading the local paper
when she suddenly said, 'There's a Show on next week.'

I was so surprised I found myself saying, 'Yes, I know.
It's at Ryechester, but there's always a huge mixed entry, and
you have to hang about a lot, and it's rather a muddle and
we usually give it a miss.'

'Let's have a look,' said Lindo, snatching the paper from
her sister. 'Um ... um ... um ... there seem to be some
rather good classes.'

I thought both of them had gone mad.

I said, 'I'm really not bothering with it. None of my
friends do.'

Melly made a face at Lindo. 'She thinks we're talking
about her silly pony races. We're talking about showing the
dogs. We always show the dogs when we get the chance.'

'Oh, dogs!' I said. 'And I wish you wouldn't talk about pony *races*, it just shows your ghastly ignorance. I might as well say you were putting Gussie and Mo in for the dog races.'

'Well, at least they *do* win something,' said Lindo. There were quite a lot of things I could have said, but I thought of Mummy and bit them back.

Melly sent for the schedule, and when it came she and Lindo pored over it for hours, deciding what they should enter the dogs for; then they filled in the form and sent it off, with the fees.

Diana Bush came round, and I told her all about this.

'Well, if they're going to Ryechester,' she said, 'why shouldn't you and I enter for one or two classes? It couldn't kill us, and it might be fun. I know it's a huge entry, and half the people look as if they'd never been on a pony before; but it probably does us good to ride with people we've never met, and what we need is experience of every kind. I'm all for it, if you are.'

I said, that after what had happened at Queen's Tracey I wasn't in the mood to make myself look idiotic again in front of Melly and Lindo; and Diana said, Don't be silly, nobody could have such bad luck twice running, and I said I hoped she was right. However in the end she persuaded me that it would be completely unsporting of me not to enter, so we grabbed hold of Melly's schedule which was still lying around, and we entered for two showing classes – one for ponies of 14.2, and the other for a best-rider-and-pony – and a Bending Race. Diana said we could scratch from the latter if there were about a million entries and it looked as if it was going to be a free fight.

On the morning of the Show Melly and Lindo started grooming the dogs as if nothing on earth else mattered.

Rapide had a slight cough, so I decided to show Black Boy, but what I did to him was nothing to what the girls did to Gussie and Mo. I always thought I was rather going it by buying a tenpenny Gleemo to wash the ponies' tails, but they had bought a terrifically de luxe concoction from the chemist's called Superba For Exquisite Hair. It was a sort of golden liquid in a handsome bottle, and it cost twenty-five pence, and though it said on the bottle that there was enough for six human shampoos, they used the lot. When Gussie and Mo emerged dripping wet they were rubbed dry, and brushed and brushed, and then – believe it or not – their topknots were set with kirbigrips.

'Well, *you* do all that silly plaiting, don't you?' said Lindo.

Then the dogs' nails had to be cut, and their eyes and ears specially washed. They looked very fed up and mournful, especially when they were bundled into a box full of clean straw. I felt so sorry for them I went and talked kindly to them, and Melly said, 'Oh, do leave them alone, Jill. I don't want them arriving all excited, or they'll never stand for showing.'

'What do they have to do?' I said.

'They have to be led out in hand at a walk, and then at a run, and then they have to stand, and *not* shake their heads about like the ponies are apparently allowed to do.'

I knew this was a slap-in-the-eye for me, but I was frightfully restrained and didn't say a thing.

Then a taxi came round, and Melly and Lindo got in with the box of dogs, and I thought I deserved a special good mark because I shouted, 'Well, cheerio and jolly good luck.'

'Oh, thanks,' said Lindo, looking a bit surprised. 'I hope you'll have good luck, too. Gosh, Melly, are you sure you've got all the grooming stuff?'

The dog classes were in the morning and the pony classes weren't until the afternoon.

Diana came round for me, and we rode slowly away.

'Ann's going to be there,' I said, 'but you know what a ghastly fusser her mother is. She won't let Ann ride because she says it's such a mixed entry and might spoil her style.' Diana said, Help! What would Mrs Derry think about *our* style? And I said gloomily, perhaps I hadn't got much to spoil in any case. Diana said, 'Oh, don't be such a Lump of Doom,' and I said, on the contrary I never felt better and Black Boy never looked better, and I couldn't care less about this Show so long as there weren't *too* many beginners floating around on half-schooled ponies, because Black Boy loathed being backed into.

'Gosh, that's nothing,' Diana said. 'Some of these kids kick. If Fantasy gets kicked I'll start a fight.'

'Good manners should be displayed at all times,' I said smugly. 'And particularly in the show ring.'

We both giggled happily as we cantered along the grass verges, and then slowed to a walk on the high road so as to arrive cool and undusty.

The first person we saw when we entered the competitors' entrance was Ann.

'Hurray!' she said. 'You've come. And you both look gorgeous, so good luck! There are quite a few people we know riding, and I do wish Mummy had let me enter. And I say, Jill, what do you think! Melly and Lindo have got two first prizes with the dogs.'

'So they ought,' I said. 'They did everything but give them home perms.'

'Let's go and see them,' Diana said. 'There's heaps of time.'

We went and got our numbers first, then we tidied up

the ponies and put their rugs on and left them in Ann's care.

In the dogs' marquee there were rows of cages, and each one had a depressed-looking dog in it. The big dogs looked bored in a sort of angry way, and the small dogs looked bored in a resigned sort of way, and the Pekes were just dead asleep. Their owners were all sitting next to them, knitting or reading *Woman*, because they were mostly women. The only dogs who were accompanied by men owners were the bull terriers and boxers, and the men were smoking pipes and dozing.

Diana and I began to giggle, because we belonged to the horsy world and it seemed so funny to find ourselves in the doggy world, rather like *Alice through the Looking Glass*. The owners looked at us too, in our spotless and spruce riding clothes, as though they couldn't quite place us.

Then we saw Melly and Lindo, with the two dogs in adjacent cages. Gussie and Mo looked completely fed up, and Melly and Lindo were still combing their hair, and there was a red rosette and a certificate fastened on each of the cages.

'What-ho!' I said. 'Nice work.'

'They both won their own class,' said Lindo, 'and Gussie got a special prize for the best non-sporting bitch.'

'Whizzo!' said Diana politely.

'Thanks frightfully,' said Melly. 'I hope you both win something.'

As we walked away Diana said that she thought Melly and Lindo were the kind of people who had a winning mentality, and their object in life was the prize and not the game, which we had always been taught was an ignoble way of thinking; and I said I agreed, and normally as long as I had had a good ride and had done my best I wasn't obsessed with cups and rosettes, but on this occasion I was feeling ignoble enough to want to win something so much I was nearly busting. I added that I knew it was unsporting, and as some poet said, 'the game is more than the player of the game, and the ship is more than the crew,' but on this occasion if I didn't have something to take home with me to show Melly and Lindo I'd give up riding and keep rabbits.

There were sixty-one competitors in the showing class, but most of them weren't much good. The ring seemed enormous, and there were hundreds of spectators standing round it, and packed stands beyond. Some of the competitors got into a muddle, found themselves going the wrong way, and were ordered out by the judges, which thinned things a little. When the calling in began I noticed that Diana, in front of me, was riding in; then another number was called, and the megaphones had to roar it out three times before I realized it was mine! I felt dumb and silly as I rode in and took my place second in line. Three others were called, and we were inspected, did our individual shows, and unsaddled. Then to my surprise I was moved up, and given the red rosette and Diana the blue. Diana grinned at me, and it dawned on me that I had won the showing class. We galloped round the ring with the rosettes, and out.

'There you are, you did it,' Diana said. 'Don't look so stunned, you mutt. You've won showing classes before.'

'The standard was pretty awful,' I said.

'Melly and Lindo won't know that.'

I felt very light-hearted and simply hugged Black Boy. In the best-rider-and-pony which came next but one, our position were reversed and Diana got first and I got second.

I felt now that all my previous disgrace was wiped out, though Ann said she didn't see what I was fussing about. The bending race was an absolute free for all, with poles on the ground and people on the ground, so Diana and I withdrew; and the judge said afterwards that he didn't blame us, and in future people would have to show some sort of qualification, such as the simple one of being able to ride, before they could enter for the competitions. This sobered everybody down, and when they put on an extra event – picking up handkerchiefs – and very few entered for it after what the judge had said, Diana and I thought we'd have a try, and I won it.

I fastened my two red rosettes and the blue one on Black Boy's browband, and collected my prizes, four pounds, two pounds, and a year's subscription to *Pony*, and felt absolutely marvellous.

'Pot-hunter!' said Diana witheringly, and I chased her half-way round the enclosure throwing grass at her. Then we gave the ponies some oats and petted them, and went off to raid the ice-cream van.

There Melly and Lindo joined us.

'I say!' said Melly, looking at me as if I was something in a shop window. 'You had some luck, hadn't you?'

'No, she didn't,' said Diana. 'She was just jolly good, and right on top of her form.'

'Don't be silly,' I said modestly. 'There wasn't any opposition, the standard was never lower.'

'I thought they all looked good, but you were the best,' said Lindo generously. 'And what do you think, Mo got another prize, in the small dogs class. So we're all going home simply loaded.'

'Look,' said Diana, 'if you two are going to be anything in the sporting world you've got to stop thinking so much about prizes. It's called pot-hunting, and by all true sportsmen is considered the depths.'

Melly said, 'But it isn't any fun if you don't win,' and Diana said, 'Really, you disgust me,' and in order to stop a row I said I'd treat them each to an extra lolly.

When we got home Mummy of course was thrilled, and showered us and the animals with congratulations, and Melly said, 'Well, at least your mother doesn't think it's less than the dust to win prizes.'

I tried to ram into her thick head the idea that prizes were all right so long as you didn't make them the be-all and end-all of your efforts, but it didn't really register.

My first task, of course, was to rush out to rub down Black Boy, rug him, feed him, thank him, and put him up for the night, and leave him happily telling Rapide about his day's adventures; but when I got back Melly and Lindo were still examining their prizes and hadn't done a thing for those two poor dogs.

'Gosh,' I said, 'I think you're the limit. What about feeding the dogs, and making them comfortable after sitting in those ghastly cages all day in front of a lot of soul-less people?'

'We're just going to,' said Lindo.

I told her she ought to have done it about an hour ago and she looked at me very coldly. It seemed as if, even in the hour of victory, we couldn't get on at all.

6

An interest in ponies

QUITE suddenly, Melly and Lindo began to show an interest in the ponies and I couldn't understand it at all. I mean, in one sense I can't understand anybody *not* taking an interest in ponies, but I thought that Melly and Lindo were hardly human, so I had given up hope of them long ago. But after Ryechester Show they were always appearing – in the stable or the orchard or wherever I was doing anything with the ponies – and watching me and asking a lot of questions, mostly silly.

Why did I do this? Why did I do that? Quite honestly I felt like saying, Use your common sense, but I was very noble and restrained. What did I feed them on? Why did I groom them when they only got dirty again? (To that one I replied with dignity, Why do you have a bath when you only get dirty again?) Why did I bother with all that stabling and grooming and feeding when there must be some hunting stables or hacking stables where they would keep them for me?

This last was just more than I could swallow. I said, 'I can't imagine why your mother keeps you around the house when there must be some orphanage nearby where they'd take you right off her hands, and save her all that pointless trouble.'

Melly said it wasn't a bit the same. They had a friend who knew all about riding, and she had an absolutely superb pony, and it lived at some local hunting stable and was ready any time she wanted it. I said, 'She must be a sordid type and I bet her pony hates her. Excuse me if I get on with my work,' and I clumped across the yard to fetch Rapide's bucket of water.

While Rapide was drinking – and if ever there was a messy drinker it is Rapide, because he sucks, thinks a minute, and then blows – they began to ask me where I got the ponies from and how much they cost.

'I expect you got them from an Arab sheikh,' said Melly, trying to be funny.

'Whose life you saved,' said Lindo. 'And he wouldn't take any payment though they are worth millions.'

I told them that I bought Black Boy for twelve pounds, from a farmer, and schooled him myself and taught him to jump. He was my very first pony, and I knew as little as he did, so actually we taught each other. I had not had Rapide very long; I had bought him from a woman called Mrs Penberthy whose daughter had outgrown him, and I had paid forty pounds for him because he was a trained pony, and if they wanted to know how I got the forty pounds they had better read a book of mine called *A Stable for Jill*, because it was all down there, and it hadn't been easy.

Lindo made the bright remark, 'Then they're not what you'd call very *good* ponies, are they?'

I controlled my fury, and said, what exactly did she mean by that? She said hastily, 'Of course I don't mean that they aren't very nice, because they are, but if you're in for showing and jumping, why not buy a frightfully good, expensive pony, and then you'd win all the time?'

I said that I knew people – such as Susan Pyke – who always rode frightfully expensive, highly-trained ponies,

and hardly ever won at all. Melly and Lindo looked as
though they didn't believe me.

I said, 'It's nearly impossible to explain to people like
you, but just because a pony costs the earth and has blood
that's practically royal blue, it doesn't say that I or any other
rider can get on that pony and soar over everything. Show
riding is just a matter of control, and understanding between
you and an intelligent pony who knows what's expected of
him. You train him yourself, and you ask of him just what
you know he can do and no more, and he rises to the occasion and he doesn't let you down, and when you don't
do well it's usually your own fault. What he cost doesn't
matter, if he's a good pony with a good head and a kind
eye and the right sort of legs. I wouldn't change Black
Boy and Rapide for the most expensive ponies in the
world, and any really horsy person would know what I
mean.'

Lindo said, 'Well, we really and truly don't know what
you mean,' and I said very sarkily, 'That doesn't surprise me,'
but it was lost on them.

I had a quick look into Rapide's ears.

'What are you doing that for?' said Melly.

'Really,' I said. 'You do ask them!'

Then Ann came round, looking awfully nice as she sat
on George, and said, 'Aren't you ready? I thought we were
going to jump some brush on the Common.'

'Gosh,' I said, 'is it that time? Melly and Lindo do nothing
but ask questions, and I can't get on at all.'

Melly and Lindo stood looking after us as we rode away,
and Ann said she thought they looked a bit longing, and I
said Rot, they despised us *and* our poor cheap ponies, and
Ann said, more fools they because they didn't know what
they were missing.

We had a wonderful canter on the Common and jumped a lot of low brush, and we were so happy we sang at the tops of our voices.

The next morning the postman looked rather laden when he arrived at our cottage, and to my surprise he handed over about ten envelopes and several small parcels. These were all addressed to Melly.

'Goodness!' said Mummy. 'It must be her birthday and we never knew. What are we going to do about it?'

She decided that directly after breakfast she would mix a cake for Melly, and then ice it for tea; but meanwhile, the two girls arrived.

Melly admitted blushingly that it was her birthday, but of course she wouldn't have thought of mentioning it. This nobility of character practically stunned me, because I certainly could not have been so restrained and polite myself. Melly opened her cards and presents, which included a bracelet from her father and mother, while I looked on with popping eyes, because the next most exciting thing to opening one's own presents is to watch somebody else opening theirs. Not that I was envious of any of Melly's presents, which were mostly handkerchiefs, bath salts, and similar sordid necessities of life, and not in my line at all; but she was very thrilled with them.

Mummy said, 'Jill feels very ashamed that she hasn't anything to give you, Melly, because she didn't know about your birthday, but do tell us what you would like – perhaps a book token or something like that – and Jill will get it for you today. We absolutely insist.'

Melly ummed and ah-ed a bit, and then went a lurid scarlet, and said that she didn't want a book token or anything like that, but what she would really like would be for me to let her have a ride on Black Boy.

I practically collapsed with surprise.

Mummy said, 'Why of course. But that's nothing at all. Jill will be delighted, won't you, Jill?'

I tried to sound delighted, and as Melly had her jeans on already, we went straight out to the orchard and I called Black Boy to come and get saddled.

'Look, Melly,' I said, 'you'll have to do as I tell you, because riding isn't just rolling on to a pony's back and jolting about like a sack of coal. Actually, I'm practically stunned that you want to try.'

Melly said okay, and she did want to try. I felt as nervous as a hen, but I started telling her how to mount, and did it once or twice myself to show her. Then she managed to get up, not too badly at all, and sat there looking all tense while I pushed her knees up and pulled her hands down and said, 'There you are. That's the position.'

Melly said it felt most uncomfortable, and I said I didn't care how uncomfortable it felt, it was right and she'd have to jolly well get used to it. I knew I was being a bit of a beast and I was surprised that Melly took it so meekly; after all, it was her birthday.

'Now make it go,' she said.

'That's up to you,' I told her. 'Gather your reins and press your knees.'

Of course, Melly grabbed the reins and pulled, and slapped in her knees as if she expected them to meet, and as Black Boy wasn't used to that kind of thing he snorted and bucked, and the next minute Melly met the ground with a resounding thud.

'Well!' she said.

'Get up,' I said. 'You're not killed.'

Melly said she'd have another try, and this time she'd sit as she wanted, and as I didn't see the point of arguing with somebody who only wanted to have a ride as a birth-day present, I said, 'Anything you like.'

I caught Black Boy, who by this time was at the end of the paddock looking offended, and brought him back, and Melly got up by herself. This time she sat well back with the reins gathered somewhere near her chest. She pushed her feet forward as far as they'd go, and said, 'This feels better.'

'I can suffer no more,' I said. 'Get on with it.'

Melly rode slowly round the paddock. When she got back she said, 'I enjoyed that.'

I told her it was more than Black Boy did, but it was her party and she could go round again if she wanted. Melly said, could she go any quicker? and I said I didn't advise it. When she got back the second time she said she quite had the hang of it, and had decided there was nothing to riding, any baby could do it. To my surprise, Lindo said, 'but you did look awful. I think Jill's way was right.'

Melly said she had copied her seat from a picture she had seen in an art gallery of a man doing a cavalry charge on a flashing-eyed charger; and I said if ever there was a cavalry charge in Chatton I'd let her know and she could join in, but it wouldn't be on Black Boy.

After that we went indoors, and as it was Melly's birth-day Mummy took us to Ryechester and we had ices at a café, and then Mummy said that Melly had better choose herself a present; so she said she'd like a writing set and we went to a stationer's shop, and Melly was about half an hour choosing between a grey one and a maroon one; but I couldn't have cared less how long she was as I had mean-while found the book department and a whole shelf of pony books, and I was up to the eyes in *Helen Rides at Hickstead* when they came and dragged me away. Mummy said she didn't think it was quite the thing to read books like that

without paying for them, in fact she would hate it if anybody did that with the children's books that she writes; and
when I confessed that I had read the first two chapters of
Helen, and the last one, and a bit in the middle, she insisted
on going back and buying the book; so I got something out
of Melly's birthday, too. In fact, I got quite a lot, because we
had the iced birthday cake for tea, and it wasn't pink and
white and kiddish, but rather sophisticated with coffee icing
and Happy Birthday done in chocolate twiddles.

I was lucky, too, because Melly didn't know any people
in Chatton so *my* friends were invited to tea, and as it rained
afterwards we stayed in and had a pony quiz. This is rather a
brainy game in which you ask people in turn questions out
of books like *Stable Management*, *Practical Show-Jumping*,
and *The Horse in Sickness and in Health*, and when anyone
fails to answer or gives the wrong answer, they have to find
the questions and ask them. Of course, when you are playing
with frightfully horse-wise people like my friends you have
to find very crafty questions to get them out. I'm afraid this
was dull for Melly and Lindo, who hadn't a clue, but were
decent in entering into the spirit of the thing; so we asked
them easy questions such as – 'Name three parts of the
horse' – for instance, pastern, fetlock, withers – and Lindo
said she could think of six; back, front, two sides, top, and
underneath, and we all shrieked.

7
The strange art of advertising

ABOUT two days later Melly walked in with a letter which she had had from her mother.

She said, 'I didn't tell you I was writing until I got the reply, but it's all right. Mummy says that Lindo and I can have a pony.'

If she had said that she and Lindo were going to have a kangaroo I couldn't have been more astounded. I said, 'But I thought you weren't interested,' and she said that up to the time of Ryechester Show they hadn't been interested, and then they had suddenly become interested and wanted to learn to ride, and they could easily manage with a pony between them. She said all this in a very matter-of-fact way.

I said, 'You paralyse me,' and she said she didn't see anything out of the ordinary in wanting a pony; and I said neither did I, if it was anybody else but her and Lindo.

I said, 'Where are you going to get one?' and she said, 'Mummy's got a friend called Mr Prescott who knows all about ponies, and he's going to see about one for us.'

I said, 'Well, nobody would "see about" a pony if it was for me, I'd want to do it all myself.'

Melly said, 'Of course we shall see for ourselves, in a way; we naturally wouldn't buy a pony unless it was one we liked.'

My pride was a bit touched, and I said I didn't see what Mr Prescott could do better than I could do myself, and I knew quite a lot about buying ponies and had always been successful with the ones I had bought; and actually – though I wasn't bragging – nobody could beat me at buying a good pony at a low price.

Melly said, what did I mean by a low price? And I said, did she want a twelve pound pony or a forty pound pony? And she snorted and said, 'Gosh, nothing as cheap and awful as that!'

This made me furious, and I said coldly, 'If you think that Rapide and Black Boy are cheap and awful, then you may be rich but you're also horrible.'

Melly said, 'Don't be so touchy, and I'm not rich and horrible, but Mummy says in her letter that if Lindo and I are going to have a pony we might as well have a first-class one that's fully trained and a good show jumper, and then we've only got to learn to ride it and we can start winning things straight away.'

I said, 'I think you're absolutely hopeless. You never think about anything but winning things. A pony isn't a machine, so that you climb on its back and it does everything right regardless of the beastly person who's holding the reins. A pony is like a person, you've got to care for it and make it care for you before you'll get any response from it at all, and that goes, however much or little you pay for it.'

Melly said quite humbly that she hadn't meant to sound beastly, and that she and Lindo were prepared to get very fond of their pony and make it fond of them, but what they wanted to be fond of was a highly trained show jumping pony, and she couldn't see anything wrong with that.

'Right ho,' I said. 'But I don't like the sound of Mr

Prescott, and if I were you I should give him a miss and put an advertisement in the County paper.'

Melly said she didn't see why Mr Prescott shouldn't be all right, in fact, he was probably marvellous; and I said I didn't see him that way at all, I saw him as a miserly old man with shifty eyes and one shoulder higher than the other, and he wore nailed boots and kept his hands in his pockets when he was talking to you, and talked out of one corner of his mouth.

By now I had got Melly thoroughly put off Mr Prescott, and my imagination was so warmed up that I added that he was probably up to the eyes in the Worn Out Horses Traffic and ought to be in prison; so in the end she said, 'Let's go and find Lindo, and I'll tell her we're not going to bother with Mr Prescott, and we'll put an advertisement in the County paper.'

Lindo agreed to this, in fact, she said, 'I'm all in favour of doing what Jill suggests. I'd much rather have the fun of buying our own pony ourselves.'

Mrs Cortman had put down Mr Prescott's address in the letter, so while Melly and I were thinking out what we should say in the advertisement, Lindo wrote a letter to Mr Prescott which said:

'Dear Mr Prescott,
Please don't bother to buy us a pony as we are getting one by ourselves.

> Yours truly,
> Melly and Lindo Cortman.'

She showed me the letter, and I said, 'I don't think that's much good. Mr Prescott will merely be horrified at the idea of your buying a pony by yourselves when you know nothing about it, and also he'll be gnashing his teeth at the thought of being done out of his ill-gotten profits, and he'll write and tell your mother, and she'll make you have Mr Prescott's choice of pony and you won't have any fun from it at all.'

Lindo saw the point of this, so together we wrote another letter.

'Dear Mr Prescott,
It is very kind of you to suggest buying a pony for us, but we are already living among some thoroughly experienced horsy people who know all about buying ponies and have placed their vast experience at our disposal, so we would like to have the pleasure of choosing our own pony under expert advice. So please don't bother any more.
Yours truly,
Melly and Lindo Cortman.'

'There!' I said. 'That ought to settle Mr Prescott. Now we'll draft the advertisement.'

Melly said, 'What we want to say is, "Absolutely first-class pony wanted. Must be fully trained and able to jump anything. Must be very good-looking and preferably grey".'

I said, 'Why grey?' and Melly said, 'It's the most showy colour,' and I said, 'I think you're the most disgusting show-off of anybody I ever met.'

Lindo said that Melly didn't mean it like that, and Melly said, 'Of course I didn't, and I really don't mind about the colour.'

Then I had a bright idea and said, 'Before we put in an advertisement, why not look and see if there's anything suitable advertised for sale in the paper?'

Melly thought that was a good idea, so I got the County

paper and found the column which says Horses and Ponies for Sale.

Lindo gave a shriek. 'Oh! Look at this. "Chestnut mare, 3 years, 14.2 h.h." – whatever that means – '

'Hands high, you idiot,' I said.

'It says, "Excellent gymkhana pony, won forty-two prizes last year. Easy to catch".'

'That settles it,' I said. 'They wouldn't have said "easy to catch" if it hadn't been practically impossible to catch. Let me have a look.'

However, Melly snatched the paper and read out: ' "Wanderlust, 5 years, 14.2 h.h. grey gelding, perfect show jumper. Lovely mover with bone and substance. Super hunter. Owner over age. £120". What on earth does "owner over age" mean?'

'I suppose it means the owner's about ninety-two,' said Melly.

'It means the owner's over sixteen and can't ride in children's classes any more,' I said. 'And you don't want a super hunter, anyway.'

'There's another one here,' said Melly. 'It says it's 12.2 but it regularly wins 14.2 jumping events, and it's steady in traffic, and – oh, blow! That's a super hunter, too. And it has played polo. But it's quiet in the stable – why shouldn't it be?'

'Give it to me,' I said, grabbing the paper. I ran my eye down the advertisements, and said, 'I think we'd better put in one of our own. We'll ask Mummy about it.'

So when Mummy came in I broke it to her gently about Melly and Lindo wanting to buy a pony, and when she had recovered from the shock we managed between us to draft an advertisement, and though the bits that Melly had insisted on putting in sounded rather boastful – such as 'only the best need apply' – we sent it off to the County paper.

I got another shock when Lindo revealed that her mother had said they could spend up to a hundred and fifty pounds on the pony. I had never been used to such opulence and it nearly stunned me, but when I came round I thought it would be rather fun for once to buy a pony in the millionaire class instead of trying to get one as cheap as possible.

I couldn't wait to tell Ann and Diana about it.

Diana said, 'We've had it, my children. Obviously Melly and Lindo are going to beat us at our own game.'

'They'll not have time if they're only here for two months,' said Ann.

'Oh, yes, they will. They'll practise night and day, and they'll be ready for Chatton Show, and win the 14.2 jumping.'

'They can't *both* ride the unfortunate pony,' I said.

'They'll ride it in turns. It'll probably be so beautiful to look at that nobody else will stand a chance in the showing classes. The judges will swoon and award it a special Cup.'

I giggled, and reminded my friends of the time that Susan Pyke showed a pony so beautiful that the judges nearly swooned, until it bit them, and then it didn't even get a prize.

Ann said, 'Well, we're silly to bother, and if we're not prepared to face any competition we can't call ourselves good horsewomen. I couldn't care less, so good luck to Melly and Lindo.'

We agreed with this.

It was three days before the advertisement appeared, during which Melly and Lindo could hardly eat for excitement. Lindo suggested that I should give them a lesson or two on Black Boy so as not to waste any time before they got their own pony; but Melly was fussy and said she didn't want to get used to any other pony but her own, as it might spoil her style.

As soon as the advertisement did appear they sat by the telephone waiting for it to ring, and believe me, within an hour it rang.

I was practising jumping over a pole jump I had arranged in the field, and as Rapide had taken a dislike to it I was trying to calm him down when Lindo came charging out.

'It's an answer to the advertisement,' she shouted. 'It sounds marvellous. It's a grey pony and very keen, and it can jump any four-foot six jump without a fault, and it's very experienced –'

'Did it tell you that itself?' I said sarkily.

'Well, you know what I mean. It was a woman called Mrs Hughes, and she lives at a place called The Meads, Little Pawley. Is that near here?'

I told her it was only about five miles away, and Lindo said, 'Oh, blow! I forgot to ask the pony's name and how many hands it had – was, I mean.'

We went into the house, and Melly and Lindo jabbered so much about this pony that you couldn't hear yourself think. What Lindo couldn't remember about the telephone conversation, Melly remembered, and it turned out that this pony had won fourteen first prizes and nine seconds the previous season, and the reason Mrs Hughes was selling it was that she was going to Canada, and she was asking only £145 for it which was a gift as, in the right hands, it would soon be winning at Wembley, Richmond, and Windsor; and they could go and see it any time they liked.

I began to feel a bit bad-tempered which I suppose was just a fit of jealousy, because I would have loved to be buying a pony for myself that would soon be winning at Wembley, etc., but I choked it down; and just then Mummy came in and the story had to begin all over again.

'Oh, do all stop talking at once!' Mummy said.

'Can we go this afternoon and see the pony?' said Melly. 'We've looked up the buses, and there's one to Little Pawley at half past two.'

Mummy said it would be foolish to be in a hurry, as there might be other replies to the advertisement; so Melly and Lindo reluctantly agreed to wait until tomorrow, and as there weren't any other replies we set out for Little Pawley the next afternoon; and all the way in the bus Melly and Lindo were asking me if I was sure if I knew how to tell if the pony was a good one, and I said, at least I knew enough to tell if he was spavined or broken-winded, and they'd better leave it at that.

8
Blue Shadow

THE Meads turned out to be a converted farm, that is, the house was still a house but the outbuildings didn't seem to have anything in them but old bicycles and garden rollers. Mrs Hughes met us at the gate, and was rather dressed up, in a pink jumper and pearls.

She said, 'I'm so glad you've come. You're going to adore Snowy.'

I thought that anybody who couldn't think of a better name for a grey pony than Snowy was lacking in imagination, if nothing worse, but I didn't say anything.

Lindo said, 'We're going to call him Little Cloud,' and I kicked her ankle and said, 'You haven't got him yet. Don't sound too keen.'

'Let's go and see him,' said Mrs Hughes. 'He's all ready and waiting for you.'

Far from being all ready and waiting for us, Snowy, who was in a small paddock, took Mrs Hughes about ten minutes to catch, and by that time she was completely puffed and didn't look very pleasant.

He certainly was a good-looking pony, and I ran my eye over him and drew imaginary lines through his shoulders and down his legs. He seemed all right, and when she caught my experienced glance, Mrs Hughes said, 'See how beautifully he stands. Now who's going to try him?'

'I am,' I said, 'though he isn't for me,' and Mrs Hughes

said, 'I can see you're a skilled rider, I expect you can jump anything,' and I said modestly, 'Not quite.'

Mrs Hughes said, 'I'll just put a saddle on him, if you'll wait a tick,' so we waited. The pony gave Mrs Hughes a bit of trouble while he was being saddled, and she said, 'Naughty, naughty.'

While Melly and Lindo looked on excitedly, I took over, and noticed that the pony had a dreamy look in his eyes which should have filled me with suspicion, but didn't. The moment I was in the saddle he began to buck violently, and the next minute I found myself thrown. I sprang up at once and looked for the pony, who with head and tail high and reins flapping was making for the fence; he jumped it without pausing – and to his credit let me add that it can't have been much less than five feet – and vanished into the market garden on the other side. By the time I got to the fence and looked over he was having a high time among the beans and cabbages.

I was furious. I went back to Mrs Hughes and the others and said, 'Either that pony's much too fresh or else he's crazy.'

'He's never, never, done such a thing before in his life,' said Mrs Hughes, looking at me accusingly, and my blood boiled.

To my horror Lindo burst into tears, and Melly said, 'It's all your fault, Jill, for pretending you can ride when you can't. We should have brought somebody who understands ponies, you've made us look such fools.'

'I like that!' I said, sizzling with indignation. 'The pony's wild.'

Mrs Hughes patted her pearls straight and said, 'He only needs an experienced rider. He's not intended for beginners.'

Mummy said, 'Excuse me, Mrs Hughes, but my daughter

is a most experienced rider and has won prizes all round the district.'

'Really?' said Mrs Hughes, and I said, 'Oh, stop it, Mummy, let's go.'

Just then who should appear but the missing and wicked Snowy, being led by a large and gaitered man, who turned out to be the owner of the market garden.

'Now then, Mrs Hughes,' he said, 'this won't do. I told you before that if I found this pony of yours among my cabbages again I'd go to court about it.' He looked at me. 'If you were thinking of buying him, miss, I can only say, don't. He's a good pony gone wrong for want of exercise, and it's going to be a tough job for anybody to handle him. He wants putting in a trap and giving a lot of work before he's fit to be ridden, and well Mrs Hughes knows it.'

'Would you take the trouble to mind your own business, Mr Chentor?' said Mrs Hughes, furiously.

'It is my business,' said the large and gaitered man calmly. 'Twenty-two cabbages and a row of beans are very much my business, and I'll want paying for them; and don't you try selling this pony to any more children without warning them, that's all I've got to say.'

That, so far as we were concerned, was the end of Snowy, and on the way home Melly and Lindo sulked and I was on my dignity.

Next morning there was a letter from a man called Mr Taylor who had seen the advertisement and had a well-trained show jumper for sale that had won prizes all last season, and had a perfect disposition, and was an absolute snip at one hundred pounds.

'Well? What are you going to do about it?' I said. 'Are you going to see it?'

'Not with you,' said Lindo.

I said, 'I think you're an unsporting beast. You know perfectly well after what that market gardener man said I wasn't in the least to blame for being thrown by that mad animal.'

'All the same,' said Melly, 'I think we need somebody more experienced. Or we might just go by ourselves and see it. We can tell whether it looks okay.'

'The owner will be surprised,' I said, 'when you can't even ride it.'

'If it has any spirit,' said Lindo, 'you probably couldn't ride it either, so sucks to you!'

'Right!' I said. 'You buy your own pony, all by yourselves. I'm just not interested.'

'You mean you're sulking,' said Lindo, 'because you couldn't ride Snowy.'

I gave a yell and picked up the nearest thing to throw at her – which happened to be the shoe brush – and it hit her on the shoulder and she screamed, and Mummy rushed in and said we all ought to be ashamed of ourselves for behaving like hooligans, and Melly said, 'We didn't do a thing, it was Jill,' and I said, 'Well, of all the beastly sneaks!' and rushed off to the orchard to console myself with the ponies.

I didn't go back to the cottage until dinner-time, and then Mummy told me that Melly and Lindo had gone off on the bus by themselves to see Mr Taylor's pony. I said I thought they were idiotic, and Mummy said she thought they were very unwise but I must learn to be more tolerant, and I said that anybody who could be tolerant towards Melly and Lindo Cortman ought to have a monument erected to them.

Just as we were finishing dinner a super car drew up at our gate and a sophisticated-looking young man in a positively glamorous green sports coat got out and walked up to the door.

The bell rang, and I said to Mummy, 'He must have got the wrong house.'

However, when I opened the door, he said at once, 'My name's Prescott. Thank you for your letter. Of course I took no notice of it, as I think you're quite mad.'

'Oh, gosh!' I said. 'Are you Mr Prescott?'

'Oh, gosh!' he said sarkily. 'Are you Miss Cortman?'

'No, I'm not,' I said. 'I'm Jill Crewe. But I thought you were quite different.'

He said, 'How different?' and I nearly told him about the shifty eyes and all the rest, but stopped in time.

'Where are these Cortman girls?' he said; and I said, 'They've gone to look at a pony. At a Mr Taylor's place. I can give you the address.'

Mr Prescott gave a hollow groan.

'Not Taylor! He's an absolute twister. I must stop them. Have you a phone?'

I asked him in, and he started wildly ringing people up. At last he turned round and mopped his manly brow, and said, 'I've stopped them. I've told them to go to the station entrance at Ryechester, and I'll pick them up there and take them to see the pony I've already chosen for them. This is putting years on me.'

I felt like saying that the Cortmans had already put years on me, and I felt about ninety. I rather liked Mr Prescott.

'They're jolly lucky,' I said, 'having such a marvellous pony bought for them. I expect there's nothing to stop them winning everything now – except of course that they can't ride.'

We both began to giggle, and Mr Prescott said, 'They'll have to go to your local riding school. This pony I've got for them is too good to spoil. I bought him yesterday from a woman I know whose daughter has out-grown him. Have you got a pony?'

'Two,' I said proudly. 'Would you like to see them?'

Mr Prescott said he would like nothing in the world so much as to see my ponies, so we went out.

He patted Black Boy and Rapide and said some nice things to them. Then he asked me where I got them, and I told him their history, which you will have read about for yourselves in my earlier books. He asked me what was my ambition, and I said, to learn dressage, and he laughed and said someday I might, and I said I hadn't any delusions about it being easy. He said he thought I was very sensible, and the basis of dressage was simply doing an absolutely perfect walk, trot, and canter, collected and extended, and anybody could practise that and they couldn't practise too much; and I said how right he was and I quite agreed, and altogether we had a very intelligent and satisfying conversation.

He then told me he had a mare called Dormella, and she could do serpentines and pirouettes when she was in the mood, and he was teaching her to change legs every four steps at a canter; and I said, 'Gosh! How super!'

He said modestly, 'I didn't say she could do it, I just said I was trying to teach her. I saw a man do it with a horse at Hickstead, but of course he was in the international class.'

I said, 'Oh, do you go to Hickstead?' and he said, not to compete, of course, just to watch; in fact, he went to Richmond and Wembley, too, but he always felt frightfully discouraged; and I said, 'You oughtn't to be discouraged, everybody has to begin some time, and you never know what you can do till you try,' and he said he had never heard such pearls of wisdom fall from anybody's mouth in his life.

Meanwhile, Mummy had joined us, and she said, 'You

really do talk rot, Jill. We'd better ask Mr Prescott to stay and have a cup of tea.'

He said, 'Tea? Good grief, what's the time! I'd forgotten all about meeting the Cortman kids. They'll have been waiting at the station for hours.'

Waiting, however, was just what Melly and Lindo had not done, because while we were standing in the hall wondering what Mr Prescott had better do, the two of them suddenly appeared and said very indignantly, 'That horrible Mr Prescott phoned and told us to meet him at Ryechester station, and he didn't turn up, so we took a taxi.'

'I'm the horrible Mr Prescott,' said Mr Prescott, stepping forth from the shadows, 'and I'm very sorry I didn't turn up, but I was talking to Jill about horses and I didn't notice the time.'

Melly's eyes went like saucers, and she said, 'You can't be Mr Prescott. Jill said you were a miserly old man who muttered out of the corner of your mouth.'

I went scarlet and could have gone through the floor, and I was furious with Melly for letting me down like that, but Mr Prescott just laughed, and said, 'But so I am, frightfully miserly, and I can mutter out of both corners of my mouth at once, which is really something.'

Lindo said, 'Have you really got us a pony? How smashing!'

Mr Prescott said, 'Yes. And mind you look after it, and learn to ride it properly, and if you want my opinion you couldn't have a better teacher for your early efforts than Jill here. She knows what she's talking about.'

This restored my self-respect quite a bit.

Melly said, 'Oh, what's it called?'

Mr Prescott said, 'It isn't an it, it's a she. And she's called Blue Shadow.'

Lindo said, 'We want to call her Little Cloud,' and Melly said, 'You do; I don't. I want to call her Superba.'

Mr Prescott said, 'You'll have to argue that out between you, but I don't see what's wrong with Blue Shadow, do you, Jill?'

I said I thought Blue Shadow was a nice name, and anyway ponies didn't like having their names changed, and I didn't see what was the point in doing so, except in the case of a sordid name like Bill or Flossie.

Lindo said, 'Okay, then, Blue Shadow it is, only I hope she isn't blue and I hope she isn't only a shadow.'

Blue Shadow arrived two days later in a horse-trailer attached to a lorry. She was very nice indeed, and I felt very envious, but tried to make my nobler feelings prevail. She was dark grey with a bluish tinge which was distinctive and unusual, and she had a white mane and tail which were quite spectacular.

'Well!' said Melly. 'We ought to win something with *her.*'

'You've got to learn to ride her first,' I suggested.

'Yes, of course,' Melly said impatiently, as if a little thing like that was hardly worth bothering about. 'I wonder how high she can jump? Mr Prescott didn't say.'

I told her that I didn't want to appear a wet blanket, but she could put high jumping out of her mind for quite a long time.

'Oh, I know, I know,' said Melly. 'But we'll be jumping her next season, if not this, and surely we'll be able to ride well enough to enter for *something* this year.'

Lindo said she knew a girl who had won a showing class after only three riding lessons, and I didn't argue, I just said, 'Well, perhaps if you work hard you'll be good enough to do that too.'

'You can try her if you like, Jill,' said Melly. 'I want to see what she looks like when she's being ridden.'

'Gosh!' I said staring. 'Me, who can't even ride!'

Melly said, 'Oh, shut up about that stupid Snowy. Let's forget it.'

Blue Shadow's tack had arrived with her, and it was really beautiful. The saddle was new and satiny in appearance; the bridle had a drop noseband, and the bit was a jointed snaffle. We took Blue Shadow to the little paddock beyond our orchard and I put the tack on her; then I mounted and adjusted the stirrups. Blue Shadow danced a little, but she soon settled down. She was a lovely ride and responded to my aids without any fuss. I took her round the paddock at a collected walk, then let her trot and canter; I thought that was enough to start with and brought her back.

'She looked marvellous,' said Lindo. 'I simply can't wait.'

Melly suddenly appeared with a double handful of oats – my oats – which she offered to Blue Shadow. The pony waffled them up very quickly.

'A lump of sugar would have done,' I said. 'Those oats cost me the earth.'

'Oh, you mingy thing!' said Melly. 'Grudging the poor darling a few miserable oats.'

I didn't say a thing. I thought I'd be tolerant for once, like Mummy said.

9
Rows, and an invitation

BLUE SHADOW was going to live at Mrs Darcy's; Mr Prescott, who knew Mrs Darcy, had settled this, and Melly and Lindo went up there to arrange about their lessons. They were considerably shaken when Mrs Darcy said, 'As you're beginners you couldn't do better than have your first lessons from Jill. I've got absolute confidence in her.'

They came back, and Melly said, 'Would you give us some lessons, please, Jill?' She sounded quite humble.

Lindo added, 'Mrs Darcy says you often teach her beginners, and of course we'll pay you, just like any other teacher.'

I saw a snag here, as I didn't think Mummy would let me take money from our guests. I was quite right, and we had a discussion about it, until Melly said, 'I'll tell you what, we'll spend the money on oats and stuff, and then it will be like a present.' I thought this was a good idea, and Mummy finally agreed to it, so we started on the lessons, though I made it clear from the first that Melly and Lindo would have to do exactly as I told them, and no trying to bait me or be clever.

I told them they ought to spend the first lesson learning how to put the tack on properly, but they jibbed at this. They wanted to ride, and the sooner the better, so I put one of them up on Blue Shadow and one on Black Boy and led them round the paddock, correcting the way they sat.

Lindo wasn't bad at all; she tried to do just as I told her, and soon sat quite nicely; but Melly still had a hankering after her cavalry charge way of sitting, and I was for ever pushing her knees up and her hands down, and trying to get her to look straight between her pony's ears instead of all round the place, as if her neck was on a swivel.

'I've got the idea now,' said Lindo smugly. 'I feel quite comfortable and I want to go faster. Melly, you look awful, and it's time I had Blue Shadow anyway.'

I went to try to help Melly to sit better, and the minute my back was turned Lindo clapped her knees to Black Boy's sides, he gave a startled side-step and Lindo found herself swinging on his neck.

'Who looks awful now?' said Melly. 'You big dope.'

Gradually, I got them sorted out and they began to improve. I couldn't say they weren't keen, in fact, they would gladly have had about six lessons a day, but I had to have a bit of time to myself to enjoy my own ponies and go out with my friends.

After I had been out one evening on Rapide I came home to find that Melly and Lindo were practising in the paddock on Black Boy and their own pony; and I was annoyed because I had already cleaned Black Boy's tack and put it away for the night.

'Oh, don't be such a fussy old thing,' said Lindo. 'We'll clean it again when we've finished.'

I said, 'I hope you will,' and of course they did, slopping the saddle soap on very wet, and using too-hot water. I told them I simply would not have my tack ruined like that (actually, they loathed cleaning tack, and if I didn't watch them they would leave it lying about dirty, and disappear) and Melly said, 'You're exactly like a horrid school-marm.'

I said I didn't mean to be, but they really were the limit,

and miles from being horsewomen; and the worst of it was that, like many beginners, the minute they found they could ride a bit they thought they were marvellous, and wanted to do advanced riding instead of practising a walk round a marked-out ring.

At this stage I told them it was time I passed them on to Mrs Darcy; so every morning they went off to the riding school and my days became comparative peace and bliss. Mrs Darcy told me they were both getting on quite well, especially Lindo who had a natural talent for riding; and though I didn't want to seem grudging I couldn't help feeling a bit low at the thought of that lovely, showy, expensive pony of theirs.

'Lindo is sure to be ready to ride her in a showing class at Chatton Show,' I said to Ann. 'It seems silly, doesn't it, to be teaching people to beat you at your own game?'

Ann said she thought I was crackers, and I never used to be like this, and what had got into me? – And whatever it was, it was time it got out; and I saw the sense of this.

We worked off our energies by making a really difficult jump in the field behind Ann's house, a double jump with a bit of everything in it, brushwood and poles and half an old stile. It looked wonderful, and Ann said all it wanted to make it quite professional was a few potted plants at the corners, like they had at Wembley. The purpose of these, Ann said, is not just for adornment but to guide the eye to the right spot, as in window-dressing. So we went along to Ann's greenhouse and hid behind the syringa bushes until the gardener had gone to his elevenses, and then we dashed in and picked out a few pots here and there where we thought they wouldn't be missed. Ann got two enormous pink begonias, and I got a eucalyptus and a bushy sort of thing with blue flowers.

When these were placed at the corners of the jumps they looked superb. We then led the ponies out to inspect them. Black Boy took one look at the begonias, tossed his head, and squealed with fright.

'Don't take any notice of him,' said Ann. 'If ever he's good enough to jump at a really high-class Show he'll have to get used to the floral arrangements, so he might as well start now.'

'Okay,' I said. 'You have first go.'

George refused twice at the first jump; then he got over with four faults, and ran right round the second jump.

Ann said, 'He isn't used to it. He'll do it properly the second time.' But George was even worse the second time.

Meanwhile, Black Boy had finished sniffing the begonias, and I put him at the jump. He cleared it, and Ann clapped madly. Black Boy, however, was so overcome to find himself faced with the eucalyptus and the blue plant that he completely refused the second jump. We spent a lot more time getting the ponies used to the floral arrangements in case they ever did jump at Wembley, and then we tried again. Neither of them could do a thing with the second jump, not even when we lowered it a bit by taking off a pole, so we decided the jumps weren't the right distance apart. This involved taking the second one down and moving it; so we did this, which took ages.

We had just finished when a shadow fell across the proceedings, and it was Ann's mother's gardener.

'Have you gone mad?' he said, holding in one hand a broken plant pot with half a begonia plant in it.

'We only borrowed them,' said Ann. 'We were going to put them back.'

'And a fat lot of them there is left to put back,' said the

gardener. 'And that there Bulowayo Elephantans was your mother's special, to go in the Flower Show next week, and I've nursed it night and day. Somebody's going to pay for this 'ere.'

'Oh, help!' said Ann, going as white as a sheet. The Bulowayo Elephantans – it wasn't that really, only it sounded like that – was the plant with the funny blue flowers, and unfortunately George had kicked it over when we weren't looking, and trodden on it.

'I should think it is, "oh, help",' said the gardener. 'I wouldn't be you when madam knows. You're not fit to be loose, you two aren't. If you was mine I'd put you in a Home. Heaven knows I've no objection to ponies if the riders is sane, but this beats all.' He picked up what was left of the blue plant and I felt so sorry for him, because he looked as if he was going to cry, and he kept on saying, 'This beats all, this does.'

'Oh, shut up!' said Ann. 'I'll go and tell Mother myself.'

I said I'd go with her, and we marched into the house and told Mrs Derry, who made the most awful fuss – being that kind of person – and brought out her usual threat about selling Ann's pony if anything like this ever happened again; and we both said how frightfully sorry we were, and Ann said she had two pounds twenty pence in her Home Bank and would pay for the plants, and Mrs Derry said, 'Don't be silly, money wouldn't buy them.'

We both felt rather awful, and a deep gloom fell upon our lives. However, when I got home I found everybody very excited, because Mr Prescott had rung up and wanted to take Melly and Lindo and me to see some really good Show Jumping next day, and would call for us in his car.

They were even more thrilled than I was, which is saying

a lot. Gus and Mo, the dogs, looked a bit longing, and I told
Melly and Lindo that since they had gone pony-mad they
were neglecting their once-adored animals; which upset
them so much that they spent the whole of the morning of
the day when we were waiting for Mr Prescott in taking the
dogs out, but it happened that Gus and Mo had got very
fond of me, and refused to go out unless I went too, which
made Melly and Lindo do a bit of thinking.

'Gosh!' I said, 'You must have hurt their feelings if they
turn to me, a total stranger, for consolation.'

Lindo, who was inclined to be weepy, actually began to
cry, and flopped down on her knees in the woods – where
we happened to be – and tried to gather both the dogs in
her arms without noticing that they had been crawling in
a swamp in the undergrowth; and when she got up Melly
shrieked, 'Oh, look at you!' and there was Lindo, covered
with green slime, all down her good grey skirt and over
her white blouse.

Lindo cried like mad, and said the whole thing was my
fault – which I thought was a bit thick – and we rushed
home to get her changed and have dinner before Mr Prescott arrived.

When Mummy saw Lindo's clothes she looked quite grim
and asked for an explanation.

Lindo said, 'I was hugging the dogs and I didn't notice
they'd been in a swamp.'

Melly said, 'It was Jill's fault for saying that we'd hurt
the dogs' feelings.'

I said, 'Oh, you are the meanest sneak I ever got stuck
with!' and Mummy said she thought it would be a good
thing if she rang Mr Prescott and told him not to come, as
we were such unpleasant girls.

We ate dinner in a thick silence until Mummy said, 'I

think it's time somebody apologized to somebody and ended this; I don't care who apologizes to whom, but we'll have this settled.'

I said it certainly wasn't my fault; and Melly said, 'I didn't have a thing to do with it,' and Lindo said, 'Oh, shut up, we're all to blame, and I apologize.'

Mummy said, 'Well, that's one decent person. Who's the next?'

I said, 'I don't mind apologizing to Lindo, but I'm not going to apologize to Melly unless she admits she was a beastly sneak.'

Mummy said she never heard of such childish behaviour; and Melly said, 'Okay, I apologize to everybody, but Jill had no business to say we'd hurt the dogs' feelings.'

I said, 'What a simple, innocent remark to start all this hoo-ha!'

Mummy said, 'Either you three go to this Horse Show as friends, or you don't go at all.'

By the time Mr Prescott arrived we had all calmed down a bit.

'I hope you won't mind us being late back, Mrs Crewe,' he said. 'This Show will probably go on till ten-thirty, and then it's an hour's drive home.'

'Eleven-thirty!' I said. 'I've never been out so late in my life. Whoops!'

Mummy said, 'It's far too late, and I ought to put my foot down, but I haven't the heart.'

As soon as we were under way in the car, Mr Prescott asked how Melly and Lindo were getting on with their riding. Melly said, 'Mrs Darcy's quite pleased with us, but as you know she's never ecstatic with anybody.'

Lindo said, 'I want to start jumping, and I don't see why I shouldn't.'

'Let's have an impartial observation, Jill,' said Mr Prescott. 'What do you think about them?'

I said, quite fairly, that they had both got on unexpectedly well, and were so keen they were working like mad at their riding; but like all beginners, they thought that once they could more or less ride they could give up doing a collected walk round the school, which was really the most important thing of all.

'Hear, hear!' said Mr Prescott; and Melly said, 'Gosh, Jill, you do talk like a schoolmarm.'

Mr Prescott said, 'She talks jolly good sense. Do you know anything about music, girls?'

Lindo said they both played the piano, and had heard Moura Lympany — who was one of their idols — several times.

Mr Prescott said, 'Right. I suppose you think a player like Moura Lympany never has to practise her scales. Well, you can bet your life that she practises them every day, for hours. And it's the same thing as taking a pony round a school at a collected walk, and a collected trot. And don't talk to me about jumping until you can canter your pony on the right leg — and I bet you didn't even know there was a right leg to canter her on, did they, Jill?'

Lindo said, 'Mrs Darcy says we'll be ready to enter for *something* at Chatton Show'; and Mr Prescott said sarkily, 'I hardly think she means the Open Jumping'; and I said, to calm things down, 'I expect they'll be able to enter a Showing Class, Melly in the under-sixteens and Lindo in the under-fourteens.'

'Come on,' said Mr Prescott. 'Let's go and have some tea. The Show doesn't begin till six.'

He took us to a sumptuous-looking restaurant, and said, 'Order what you like.'

I blinked, and said, 'Do you honestly mean, what we like? I mean, Mummy usually chooses, and it's scones and cakes.'

Mr Prescott said, 'That sounds pretty dull to me. I thought schoolgirls liked sausages and chips and banana splits, but forgive me if I'm wrong.'

I practically swooned at the gorgeous idea of sausages and chips and banana splits at half-past four in the afternoon; but, believe it or not, that is what we had; and Lindo and I had ice-cream sodas to drink with our meal, but Melly went all sophisticated and had coffee.

By the time we found ourselves in our seats in the huge arena we were nearly delirious, and I wished with all my heart that I had Ann or Diana or one of my real, horsy friends with me to share this thrill. The jumps looked to me both varied and colossal, and there was an army of attendants busy on the ground.

'Well, what do you think of this set-up, Jill?' Mr Prescott asked.

I said I thought it was absolutely splendiferous and supersonic.

'How would you like to have a go round the course with your Black Boy?'

I said, 'I'd love to, if there wasn't anybody watching; only the jumps look frightfully high.'

'They're only four-foot sixes,' he said, 'with perhaps a couple of five-footers, but for jumping off they're liable to go up to six foot or over. Of course, some of them have an enormous spread, and they're all definitely tricky; that four-foot-six pole, for example, with nothing below to judge it by.'

Melly said, 'Have you ever jumped a course like this yourself?' and Mr Prescott blushingly replied that he had, so we fired questions at him and it was revealed that he had actually once won Silver Spurs at Windsor, whereupon I nearly swooned, not having realized what a terrific person he was. However, I quickly regained enough presence of mind to ask him for his autograph.

The first jumping competition began and went on for an hour and a half, which seemed to me about ten minutes. Some of the horses and riders had famous names, but they didn't always do so well, which was encouraging to anybody like me. One is apt to get the idea that a marvellous horse and a marvellous rider leave nobody else in the competition with any chance at all, but such, dear readers, is not the case. This whole competition was a series of breathless hushes and gasps, and every time a horse nearly did a clear round and then brought the last pole down the whole enormous crowd said, 'Ooooh!'

'Oh, Golly!' I said, when it was over. 'I feel so worn out, as if I'd been round all those jumps fifty times myself.'

'I wish I owned the horse that won,' said Melly. 'Wasn't it super? And it carried its tail stuck out like a banner.'

'That's just the way it's tail's plaited,' said Lindo. 'It couldn't very well do anything else. I liked the way it gave a little flick to its back feet as it went over each jump; that helped it. Oh, do you think we could possibly teach Blue Shadow to flick her feet like that, Mr Prescott?'

Mr Prescott said in a rather damping way that as Lindo was only just learning to canter – usually on the wrong leg – it would be quite a long time before we need discuss what to do about Blue Shadow's heels over a five foot jump.

10
An awfully queer
paper chase

IT took just about five minutes to clear away all those
enormous jumps. This seemed to me a miracle when I
thought that it took us practically a whole day to clear away
the jumps in Ann Derry's field; but of course our jumps were
made of bits of wood and branches of trees and rather messy
brush and other sordid things, and there were only two or
three of us working, while these jumps were made of beautifully fitting pieces and there were dozens of men all working
at once.

The next item was an exhibition of dressage by a Swedish
officer. The mare he rode was like a ballet dancer; she did the
most fascinating things with her legs.

Mr Prescott said, 'Now I don't want a squeak out of
any of you while I'm watching this, so the first one who
says, "What's he doing that for?" will be quickly and
silently murdered.'

We watched the incredible exhibition in silence, while
the commentator warbled on about full-passes and serpentines and *passage* – which in case you don't know, is the
name of a difficult movement – and I nearly burst trying not
to ask Mr Prescott questions.

Then there was another very exciting jumping competition, in which the competitors chose their own seven jumps

out of twelve, and gained the number of points that the
jumps were valued at. There was a jump-off at the end of this
competition which went on for four rounds between three
horses, each time the jumps being raised. The horse we were
most interested in was a lovely little mare of only 15.2
hands. She jumped like a cat and the whole crowd adored
her, because she was so little compared with the other
horses, and so plucky. The commentator announced, 'This
is the final jump-off. If all three competitors still get clear
rounds the prize will be divided.'

We all held our breath. The first horse got four faults at
the first jump; the second horse got four faults at the third
jump – they were only jumping three – and then the little
mare came in with her ears pricked and her eyes shining,
and went over all three jumps like a bird. She had won!
I think you could have heard the cheering ten miles away.

Then all the winners lined up under the flood-lights to
receive their prizes from the Duchess of somewhere or
other. Mr Prescott said that at Hickstead and Wembley the
Queen sometimes presented the Cups and prizes.

By now, I simply was not there at all. I was in a sort of
beautiful golden dream. I was giving a dressage exhibition
in a huge magnificent arena, under the arc lamps, on a
horse that did intricate steps like a ballerina. It was so still
you could have heard a pin drop, except for occasional
Ooohs and Aaahs of admiration which the crowd could not
repress. Riding this horse was like floating on a cloud. Then
the scene changed and I was jumping six foot jumps with
the greatest of ease, simply soaring over, and the crowd
was clapping, and I had done a final clear round; and then
I was all alone in the arena and the Queen in a most glamorous blue dress was handing me a Cup, and the photographers were snapping madly.

'Do you want to spend the night here by yourself?' said Melly's voice. 'Or have you sat on some gum?'

I realised that nearly everybody had gone, and that my party had got to the exit before they realized I wasn't with them, and looking back they saw me still glued to my seat with my mouth open and a faraway look in my eyes.

Lindo said, 'People must have thought you weren't quite all there, Jill;' but Mr Prescott gave me a very sympathetic look as though he understood, and sometimes had beautiful golden dreams of his own.

The result of going to this Show was that Melly and Lindo practised their riding like mad. They practised on Blue Shadow and one of the riding school ponies, and on Black Boy, when I let them. Actually, it didn't do Black Boy any harm because they were both careful riders, but neither of them could do a thing with Rapide. The reason for this was as follows.

We were all up at the riding school when Melly said she would like to try Rapide. She didn't manage at all well, and came back with a red face, saying, 'He's a hopeless pony. He feels like a rocking horse, and when I give the aids he just puts his ears back and nothing happens.'

I couldn't be bothered to argue with her, so I said, 'Okay, don't bother with him any more, only please don't make insulting remarks about him to his face, because he can understand every word you say.'

Melly said, 'You really are bats, Jill,' and Lindo said, 'Can I ride Rapide in the half-past ten class?' I knew she said this because she didn't like to think there was a pony she couldn't ride; also she wanted to go one better than Melly.

So I told her she could.

Mrs Darcy had the class riding round in a circle. Poor old Rapide looked far from happy with Lindo. His neck was stiff and his jaw set, and Lindo was pulling furiously to prevent him pressing the pony in front.

'Try and keep your distance, Lindo,' Mrs Darcy said.

'I can't,' said Lindo in an annoyed voice.

I saw Rapide's ears go back. The next minute Lindo used her heels very hard, in fact, she kicked Rapide. He ran back, reared, and the pony behind gave a terrified squeal and began to limp.

'Stop everybody!' said Mrs Darcy. She then began to tell Lindo off. Lindo said she hadn't kicked Rapide, she had merely used her heels. Mrs Darcy said sarkily, 'And I suppose if you had merely had a stick you would have merely used that too? Not likely! Not in my riding school!'

I knew this was about the worst thing Mrs Darcy could say, because she was dead against the use of sticks. Anyway, Lindo blamed the whole episode on Rapide, not on her own inefficient riding, so both she and Melly refused to have anything more to do with him; which didn't worry me, except that I boiled at the thought of Rapide's feelings being hurt, because he is a pony who needs understanding, and when you understand him he will do anything for you.

I think Lindo was a bit ashamed of the idea that there was a pony she couldn't ride, because after that she practised her circle work doggedly and improved very quickly.

Meanwhile, some of my friends were taking rather a dim view of the fact that I was tied up so much with the Cortmans. Ann said, 'We never seem to do anything now that's any fun. Can't we get something up?'

Diana Bush said, 'What sort of a something? Most of the things we get up seem to end in disaster.'

Val Heath said, 'Couldn't we have a picnic ride? We haven't had one for ages,' and Ann said, 'Well, you know what happens when we have a picnic ride. We only get as far as the woods, and then everybody is so jolly greedy they start wanting the picnic, and we eat and eat, and then we come back.'

Val said, 'I wonder if I could get my father to lay us a paper trail. It would be rather fun, and we should have to follow the course to the end, and we could have a time limit.'

'And prizes?' said Pam Derry.

'Oh, gosh, don't you ever think about anything but prizes?' I said. 'Anyway, who's going to give prizes?'

'My father might,' said Val, 'if he thought it would encourage us to be keen. He's always talking about being keen, and giving the horses a work-out, and that sort of thing. He says I stay in bed too jolly late in the morning ever to be a real horsewoman.'

'Well, let's have the paper chase about five o'clock in the morning,' said Diana, who was one of those people who like getting up; and everybody else gave a yell of horror.

Val's father, when approached, said he would like very much to lay us a paper trail, and we all got excited about it. One or two people's mothers, of course, began to fuss and say, was it perfectly safe? and Val said, if it was perfectly safe it wouldn't be any fun, which caused quite a stir in the dove-cotes; but at last all the fond parents were either calmed down or stunned into silence, and the paper chase was on.

Melly and Lindo both wanted to go.

Mummy said to me, 'Do you really think they're up to it?' and I said, 'Well, they're both unequalled at hanging on, either in the saddle or round the pony's neck; but the point is, I'm lending Black Boy to a cousin of Val's who's coming over specially for the ride and hasn't her pony with her, and I'm going to ride Rapide myself, so there's only Blue Shadow between Melly and Lindo. They'll have to fight it out.'

Melly said, 'We'll settle it in a perfectly civilized way by tossing a penny.'

So they got a penny and tossed it, and Lindo said Heads, and it came Heads. Melly said, she meant the best out of three, and Lindo said, 'You beastly swizz!' and then they ceased to be perfectly civilized and began to quarrel madly.

Mummy took the penny and said, 'This one settles it. Call, Melly.' Melly said Tails, and it came Tails, and Lindo went very dignified and said, 'I don't care. I'd rather take the dogs out anyway.'

The day of the paper chase turned out to be one of those days when the weather doesn't know what it intends to do. There were gusty showers and then bursts of sunshine, and Mummy said we were to ride in our macs. I didn't mind much, but Melly was furious because she had got herself up in her new jodhpurs and a frightfully smart jacket and some new yellow gloves, and she said her mac was shabby and the wrong colour and spoilt it all, but Mummy just said, No mac, no go. So we rode off to Halfpenny Bottom where we were all to meet.

Seventeen people turned up, and a boy called Walter Richards pointed to a grassy track that ran up towards the woods and cried dramatically, 'There lies the trail!' and went pounding off at a gallop; and everybody streaked after him, and Melly said, 'If they're going to gallop like that I shall get left behind, because I simply can't,' and I said, 'Don't worry, just canter; they'll have to slow down when they get to the woods.'

Val Heath's father had been clever and had dropped the paper clues quite far apart, so you had to do a bit of searching round. The trail ran right through the woods and then cunningly turned back on itself, and skirted the Common and set off up Dinglefold Lane towards the wilder country

of the Downs. The gusty showers still kept coming; but by
now Melly had discarded her mac and tied it to her saddle
by the belt, and she was very wet but had the consolation of
looking terribly smart, though I don't know who *that* would
impress.

I was enjoying myself. I didn't bother about getting up
among the leaders, but listened contentedly to the gay
shouts of View Halloo-o-o as the trail was picked up. It was
gorgeous to be riding over the open country and under the
enormous sky, with the wind blowing in my face, and
Rapide as keen and happy as I was myself.

Melly called out, 'Oh, goodness, look! They're jumping a
fence. What am I going to do?'

I said, 'Just ride round and come back to us,' and she
managed to do this. The next time there was a jump the same
thing happened, Melly rode round; but the third time I
waited and Melly didn't come up. The jump had been an
easy one and the field was streaming away ahead. On one
side was a small copse, and the other way — from which I
expected Melly to come — lay fields with high hedges. I rode
along the fence I had just jumped, and yelled 'Melly, Melly,
Melly!' I wondered what on earth she was doing. Then I
realized that the fence was very long, and there wasn't a
gate anywhere near. When finally I did reach the end of the
fence I had to jump a hedge, and there was Melly, sitting on
the ground in a sort of dingle, and Blue Shadow standing
by looking sorry for herself, with the saddle underneath
her and her feet all tangled up in the reins.

'What on earth happened to you?' I said.

Melly said that she hadn't been able to find a gate, so
she'd tried to jump the hedge — bearing in mind the fact
that she'd never jumped anything higher than a pole on
two bricks — and she thought the girth must have

broken, because Blue Shadow had sort of come to pieces.

'Anyway, I'm back where I started,' said Melly, 'and I've hurt my funnybone.'

'Get up,' I said, 'and let's have a look at you.'

Melly got up and didn't seem much the worse.

'Come on,' I said. 'Let's get this tack off, and see what we can do.' What had happened was that the girth hadn't been properly fastened and had broken away from the buckle. I was so annoyed that I told Melly off. I said that people who couldn't be bothered to put on their tack properly didn't deserve to have ponies at all, and I couldn't be watching her *all* the time to see that she saddled up correctly, she ought to know how by now.

To my surprise, Melly said quite humbly, 'It was my fault. I was in a hurry, and I thought it would do. I'm awfully sorry, Jill.'

'Okay,' I said. 'We all learn by our mistakes. I can put this right, I've got some straps and things in my saddle-bag.' I began to work, and Melly looked so miserable that I couldn't be beastly to her; and finally I found a rather old Mars Bar in the bottom of the saddle-bag and we shared it.

By the time I'd finished the job I realized that the paper chase would now be about two miles away. I said, 'I suppose we'll have to go home!'

'But I don't know where we are,' said Melly.

I said, Neither did I, but there wasn't any point in stating the obvious. I helped her up on Blue Shadow, and I swung myself up on Rapide and we began to ride through the dingle in search of a gate. There were a lot of brambles, and the ponies loathed them and became rather nappy. Melly set her teeth and hung on like grim death.

At last we came to a gate which opened on to a cart track. We followed it, and it widened into a lane, and after about a quarter of a mile it opened on a main road down which lorries marked 20 m.p.h. were zipping along at about fifty.

'Oh, I can't,' said Melly. 'I've never ridden in traffic.'

I saw the force of this. I had a vague idea of leading Blue Shadow, but I didn't think it would work, as I didn't know her very well and she might bolt; also, Melly wasn't a person of outstanding sense with whom to be caught in an awkward situation; so I said, 'We'd better turn back into the country and find some field path.'

We wandered about rather aimlessly. At last Melly said, 'Here's a gate and a lovely field.'

'Come on, then,' I said, 'and keep round the edge. We're trespassing, anyway, but it doesn't look so bad if you're not prancing all over the field; the farmer can see we're merely lost.'

Melly said she thought 'merely lost' was good, considering we were what she'd call colossally lost; and just at that moment we saw the bull. He was about thirty yards away, rising slowly to his feet and staring at us.

Melly gave a yelp.

'Shut up,' I said. 'Don't attract his attention.'

'But it is attracted,' she said. 'Oh, Jill, it's like that awful film we saw of the bull fight. Gosh, what are we going to do when he charges?'

I knew that a bull who might disregard a person walking would nearly always go for a horse. I said, 'I'll try and draw him off, Melly. You ride back quietly to the gate, and shut up and don't argue. Get going.'

I leaned over and caught Blue Shadow's rein and turned her, then I gave her a cut with my stick; but she had seen the bull and let out a wild whinny.

I bounced up and down in my saddle and yelled, and the

bull whose eyes had been fixed on Blue Shadow swivelled them round to me.

Melly was now on her way to the gate. I collected Rapide and set him straight for the opposite hedge.

'Come on, boy,' I said. 'And please have some sense and don't let me down.'

From the tail of my eye I saw the bull begin to lumber towards us. I hadn't a doubt about Rapide's speed, but I measured the approaching hedge with more than a spot of misgiving. It was every bit of four-foot six, dense and bristly, and Rapide was used to tidy jumps and knowing what was on the other side of them. I didn't dare think what would happen if he refused or failed to clear. I patted his neck as we raced for the hedge, and felt hesitation run along his shoulder. Then I used the stick, which was a thing I rarely did, and put him right at the jump, thinking, Gosh, it's now or never!

He didn't refuse, he went straight for it, and the next minute we were in the air and coming down on the other side with bits of hedge stuck all over us. Rapide fell on his knees and I went over his head. Then we both got up, and I said, 'Phew!' We were in a field of oats.

11
Blue paint

'GOLLY, you were heroic!' said Melly, as she appeared leading Blue Shadow.

'Don't you dare tell them a word of this at home,' I said. 'But Rapide did the jump of his life. He was absolutely marvellous.' I hugged and patted Rapide, and began to examine his knees which were quite all right; in fact, he was in better shape than I was, because my shoulder hurt like mad and the jump had nearly pulled my arms out of their sockets. Rapide nuzzled my face, and I said, 'I'd give anything if I had a lump of sugar for him. I wish we hadn't eaten that Mars Bar.'

Melly said, 'Well, give him a few oats,' and I said, 'Gosh, you can't go pulling up people's oats for your ponies,' but Melly had already got a handful which Rapide accepted and munched happily, with a very smug expression. He then pulled a lot of faces at Melly, which he only did when he was pleased with people.

'What do we do now?' Melly asked.

I said that we'd better try and find some human being and ask our way home. We rode for quite a long way, but it must have been tea-break or something because there wasn't a soul about. I thought this was rather odd and just like life; because if ever you are in the mood to have miles of countryside entirely to yourself and are feeling poetic, every hedgerow and field seems to be bristling with sons of the soil doing their sordid but necessary toil of ditching or ploughing or whatever it is they do.

At last I decided that we had better approach a farm and ask the way, so we rode into the nearest yard, which needless to say was quite deserted. I opened the door of the biggest outhouse and walked in, to find myself in the midst of a hen battery. The electric light was on, and all the hens were sitting in their cages row upon row, with a sort of Hope-Is-Dead expression on their faces, like criminals in those prison films. It all looked very industrial and sordid, and there was a solemn hush, which I broke when I spotted a man bending over a bucket, and said, 'Excuse me, but can you tell us the way back to Chatton?'

Melly said, 'Actually, we've been roving about for ages –' so I gave her a sharp kick on the ankle, because statements like that are no way to inspire a farmer's confidence, and said, 'Of course we've been very careful not to do any damage.'

The man looked at us and said, 'Riding, are you?'

I thought that would have been obvious, but he was evidently one of those simple sons of the soil who like to express an idea plainly.

'I'll come and put you on the way,' he said, and I said, 'Thank you very much.'

He then fiddled with one of the hen's cages, and I could not resist saying, 'I think hen batteries are cruel.'

He said, 'What for? Look at them, they're happy, ain't they? You can tell by their expressions.'

I said, that was just it, they hadn't any expressions beyond one of half-witted despair; not that free hens' faces actually light up when you talk to them, but there is a gleam.

He looked impressed and said he'd think it over, but he still felt that battery hens had an absolutely carefree life, and that was something.

Just then a bell tinkled somewhere in the remote fast-nesses of the farm, and the farmer said, 'That's tea. You'd better come in and have a cup with the old lady. My Mum.'

We went into the farmhouse. 'My Mum' turned out to be a beaky old woman of about one hundred who looked at us in our jodhpurs and said, 'Huh! Young women riding in trousers. Huh! Not in my day. Huh!'

To my horror Melly got the giggles and had to smother her face in her hanky. The old woman said, 'What's the matter with your friend, huh? Is she being sick, huh?'

This nearly finished me off, I started coughing madly so as not to shriek with laughing, and the farmer came in with four cups of tea on a tray and four enormous slices of fruit cake. Somehow we managed to get this down, and I said, 'We'd better be going now, if you don't mind.'

Melly said, 'Thank you very much for the tea,' which was thoughtful of her, and we went out into the yard and untied the ponies from the pump where we had previously tied them up.

The farmer said, 'You wouldn't be with that lot that was paper-chasing?'

'Oh, yes, we are,' said Melly. 'Have you seen them?'

The farmer gave a sort of snort. 'Oh, yes, I've seen them,' he said. 'I moved the paper and sent them the wrong way. Ha-ha.' He roared with laughing.

'Gosh!' I said.

'But I'll send you two the right way,' he said. 'Come on.'

We followed him between some pigsties and into a grassy track, and in few minutes we saw the paper trail.

'Keep right on,' he said. 'When you get to the tree that was struck by lightning, turn left, and when you get to the duck-pond – the big duck-pond, not the little duck-pond –

turn right and you'll be in Dogrose Lane. Follow your nose and you'll get to Chatton. It's about four miles.'

We rode on. Melly said, 'If we remember all that we'll get *somewhere.*'

The farmer's four miles proved to be under-estimated. We had been riding for practically one hour when I found out where we were, and at the same moment we came up with the tail of the paper chase.

'Hullo,' said a boy called Hugh Prior. 'Some bounder of a farmer put us on the wrong track and we've been going round in circles. We lost the trail and never found it again.'

'We've had a simply terrific adventure – ' began Melly, and I glared at her. She shut up.

'What happened?' asked Diana Bush.

I gave Melly the look of a hungry Siberian wolf in hot pursuit of the fleeing moujiks, and she said, 'Well, we got into a hen battery and the farmer gave us a cup of tea.'

'Crumbs!' said Diana. 'Call that an adventure!'

Eventually the whole pack of us arrived back at Val Heath's house more or less together, and Mr Heath said, 'I expected you hours ago. The time is very bad, and I wouldn't know who to give prizes to if there were any, so you'd better all have some buns and cake and call it a day.'

Everybody looked very wet, and some people were scratched, and they were all talking at once about the various adventures they had had.

Melly and I rode home, and I said, 'Once more, not a word about You Know What!'

She said, 'It's an awful shame really, because Rapide did jump about five foot and you can't even talk about it. Is your shoulder all right now?'

I told her it still felt a bit hot, but I'd get over it.

However, all the excitement of the day was not at an

end, because when we got home Lindo rushed out and said, 'I've been frightfully busy. Guess what I've done?'

We still had the ponies to rub down and feed, so I said rather grumpily, 'You might come and give us a hand.'

'Okay,' said Lindo. 'I'll do Blue Shadow, only do come and see what I've done.'

We very soon saw what Lindo had done. It happened that I had said a few days before that I intended to paint the stable door when I had time, and Lindo being on her own decided that she'd give me a surprise, so she went down to town and bought a huge tin of paint and a brush and started to amuse herself. The colour of the paint, I may add, was a bright and vicious blue. She had done the stable door, and then – you know what it is when you've got paint – she had to go on to paint everything in sight! She'd painted the window frames and the window sills, and the wooden partition between the two stalls, and the mangers, and about half the floor – which was accidental, as the tin tipped over. She'd also painted the gate into the orchard, and as much of the fence as she could manage before the paint gave out.

It was all so blue it made you reel. Everywhere you looked you could see nothing but blue. What was worse, it was all sopping wet, as she'd put too much on and it wasn't the quick-drying sort, anyway. When I took Rapide in, his feet stuck on the blue stable floor; he pulled himself free and his flank caught the blue partition, leaving a long blue streak. He gave a startled whinny, snatched at some hay, and got a wet blue mouthful which he spat out, and bucked angrily. I had a job to calm him. The smell of paint was sickening.

'Well, now you've done it!' I said to Lindo furiously. 'You must have gone blue mad. You really are absolutely hopeless!'

'I only wanted to please you,' she said. 'I thought it would have dried.'

'Well, it hasn't,' I said, leading Rapide out into the yard. 'Rapide's hot, and I'll have to leave him outside, and he'll get pneumonia and die. I wish you'd never come here, you horrible little beast.'

Just then Val Heath, whose cousin had been riding my other pony, turned up with Black Boy.

'Oh, my Russian Aunt!' she said. 'What's going on?'

Melly said, 'Lindo painted Jill's stable for her, and Jill's being beastly about it, and I think it was jolly decent of Lindo to try, even if it is a bit wet.'

'Wet!' I said. 'You can smell it a mile off, and it's too cold for Rapide to stay out all night, and – look out!'

It was too late. Black Boy had ambled up to the orchard gate as he always did, and tried to push it open with his nose. He leapt back, rolling his eyes, and there was blue paint all over his face.

Lindo burst into tears and began to cry noisily; Melly rushed to her aid, glared at me, and said, 'I simply hate you.'

I said, 'I wish I hadn't saved your life,' and Val said, 'What are you talking about?' and I said, 'Oh, nothing.'

Melly said, 'I don't really hate you, of course, but I think you're being mean to Lindo, because she thought she was going to please you. She didn't know the horrible stuff wouldn't dry, and it doesn't look such a revolting colour in the tin, so how could she know? I think you ought to jolly well beg her pardon.'

I said bitterly, 'I like that! I think she ought to jolly well beg mine. Supposing I'd plastered Blue Shadow with loathsome paint, you'd have had plenty to say; but of course I don't descend to the depths of idiocy that you two descend to.'

'Look,' said Val. 'This argument will go on all night. I'll tell you what, I'll take your two ponies home with me, Jill, we've got plenty of room. Dad will get the paint off them, and settle them down.'

I said, 'That's awfully decent of you, Val. Thank goodness, I've got *some* friends.'

Val rode off, leading my two ponies, and I stalked into the house. My shoulder was hurting and I felt dirty and tired, but not hungry, owing to having had two teas.

Mummy was typing madly in her room with the door open. As I went by she called out, 'Is that you, Jill? Did you have a nice run?'

'Not bad,' I said. 'Everybody got lost.'

She said, 'Where are Melly and Lindo?'

I said, 'They're out in the yard.'

I barged into my room and started pulling off my clothes and hurling them all over the place, then I dragged on my dressing-gown and rushed into the bathroom and started the hot water running. I splashed in the bath feeling as mad as a wild hyena.

By the time I came out Mummy had discovered what Lindo had done.

'I was out,' she explained, 'or of course I wouldn't have let her do it.'

'She's ruined everything,' I said. 'She's ruined my stable and my orchard gate and fence, and everybody will be talking about it and laughing at me because my ponies have got blue paint all over them. I loathe the Cortmans and I never want to see them again.'

Mummy said, 'Lindo meant well. She wanted to please you. She didn't make a fuss when she was left out of the ride, and she thought that while you were away she'd do something useful.'

'Useful!' I snorted.

'It's a funny thing,' said Mummy, 'but I seem to remember somebody else who did a lot of things that were meant to turn out well, and turned out very badly indeed for other people. But the people affected were rather decent and understanding about it. For instance, there was a certain Bring and Buy Sale where some things of mine got sold by mistake, things I valued. Perhaps I needn't say any more.'

I felt very small and mere and wormlike. Looking back on my purple past I realized that practically everything I had ever done had caused somebody else a lot of trouble, and yet those other people had never said they loathed me and never wanted to see me again.

'Okay,' I said. 'I get it. Where is Lindo?'

'In the kitchen,' said Mummy. 'Crying.'

I went downstairs in my dressing-gown. Lindo was sitting on the kitchen floor nursing both the dogs and gulping into their fur.

'It's all right, Lindo,' I said. 'I was a beast, because you meant to please me, and it got messed up. Well, I've done the same thing myself, so let's call the row off.'

'Oh,' said Lindo, sniffing madly. 'What did you paint?'

'I didn't paint anything, you idiot,' I said. 'Come on, let's get supper ready.'

Melly and I kept our grim secret about the bull. I mean, Mummy would have had fourteen fits and would have stopped me doing any cross-country riding, and anyway I had learned my lesson about entering strange fields. Don't you do it either! The blue paint dried, and the wind and sun took some of the blueness out of it, so it wasn't so bad after all.

12
What a gymkhana!

THE row died down, and to please Mummy I tried to be especially nice to Melly and Lindo but nearly burst in the process. They had suddenly become very gymkhana conscious, and did nothing but ask when they would be able to enter for something. In the end Mrs Darcy said, 'Oh, let's push them in for a showing class somewhere. Either they'll win and feel better, or they'll lose and be taken down several pegs, so whatever happens they'll be easier for you to live with, Jill.'

So we chose a small gymkhana that was being held for charitable purposes in the field behind the Rectory, and we entered Melly riding Blue Shadow in the under-sixteen class, and Lindo riding Blue Shadow in the under-fourteen class.

Gosh, the way they went on you would think that nobody had ever entered for a showing class before! They were out every day on the Common practising.

'When we're ready you might come and watch us,' said Lindo.

'And give us some tips,' said Melly. 'The important thing is, we've got to do a good individual show.'

'Don't be silly,' I said. 'The gymkhana is only a small affair, and most of the people in the showing classes will be practically beginners, like yourselves. As long as you can sit straight and not actually hang on the pony's neck, and as long as the pony isn't actually bow-legged, you'll stand as good a chance as anybody. You've been better taught than most people, that's one thing.'

'And of course you've got a supersonic pony,' said my friend Diana Bush, who was with us at the time. 'She's show-trained and used to the game, and she looks so beautiful and prizeworthy that the judges will be falling flat on their noses to call her in.'

I couldn't help sighing with envy every time I looked at Blue Shadow. Of course, I adored my own two ponies; but who hasn't dreamed of riding a pony as beautiful as the day and frightfully expensive and a trained show-jumper into the bargain? Blue Shadow looked so proud and so perfect; and there she was being ridden by two beginners, and entered for a potty little gymkhana where there wouldn't be another pony within miles of her for looks and cleverness.

'All you two goons have got to do,' I said, 'is to sit up straight and keep your hands down and let the pony do the rest. It's a piece of cake, and quite honestly I feel we're being rather unfair to the farmers' kids in letting you enter at all.'

'Oh, don't worry,' said Lindo. 'This is just the start. We'll soon be in the big-time classes and then we'll really win things.'

'You beastly little pot-hunter!' said Diana. 'I hope you get the sort of judge who isn't dazzled by a super pony. If I was a judge I'd pick out a not very good pony who'd been thoroughly well schooled by its owner, and I'd look for a rider in old jodhs and a patched jacket who looked as if she loved riding for its own sake. Thank goodness, some judges do.'

'We can't help it if our clothes are new,' said Melly.

'No, but you can help looking like a shop-window model of What The Well-dressed Child-rider Ought to Wear,' said Diana.

'Oh, shut up about us,' said Lindo.

'Oh, go and throw mud on yourselves!' said Diana.

'No, but honestly,' said Melly, 'just watch me ride round the ring, and tell me if it isn't rather good. Do, Jill.'

'Okay,' I said. 'Get on with it.'

Melly mounted Blue Shadow in a rather sloppy way and walked her out. The next minute she was cantering showily round an imaginary ring. She came back with a sort of flourish and slid down.

'How's that?'

'Well, in the first place,' I said, 'you won't get away with mounting like that, not if the judges have got eyes. With a pony like Blue Shadow, who stands like a rock and is too much of a lady to show resentment, you can get away with murder; but if you do that with a nappy pony it'll side-step and leave you flat.'

'And in the second place,' said Diana, 'you can't go straight from a walk into a canter.'

'But I can,' said Melly.

'Give me strength!' said Diana. 'You're not in a circus. And another thing, you went round all the corners on the wrong leg. If you were in a jumping competition you'd have your pony right off balance and she couldn't jump a thing.'

'Yes, Diana's right,' said Lindo. '*I'm* absolutely perfect on legs.'

'She's absolutely perfect on legs!' I chanted, and Diana and I yelled in unison, 'Give me strength!'

'Well, I am,' said Lindo smugly. 'And I've started working with my stirrups crossed.'

'We can't teach these two anything,' I said. 'It'll be heaven help all the other competitors when they get going.'

Melly and Lindo remained terribly confident until the actual morning of the gymkhana; then they went completely to pieces.

'Oh, I wish I hadn't entered,' wailed Melly. 'Oh, I'm absolutely terrified. I know I shall fall off, or crouch, or do something awful.'

'Oh, Jill, I feel quite numb already,' said Lindo, 'so what shall I be like when millions of people are looking at me? Supposing I drop the reins?'

I felt much more well-disposed towards the Cortmans now they were in this mood of humility, so I said kindly, 'Everybody feels like that at their first gymkhana. It's an absolutely paralysing feeling, but the minute you get into the ring you're all right. Truly you are.'

'I can't believe it,' said Melly. 'Everybody will laugh at me. What if Blue Shadow starts to graze? I wouldn't know what to do.'

I said that Blue Shadow was much too well trained to do anything of the kind.

'Just pretend you're having a ride on the Common,' I said, and Lindo said, 'What a hope! With all those millions of people staring at us.'

I said there wouldn't be millions, only about two or three hundred, and they'd all be fathers and mothers who hadn't any eyes except for their own kids, but Melly and Lindo wouldn't be soothed and went on drooping round the kitchen and moaning as if they were going to have nineteen teeth out.

'If you feel like that,' I suggested, 'you'd better scratch from the gymkhana altogether.'

Strangely enough, that was all they needed to buck them up. Oh, no, they wouldn't think of scratching; they were in it, and they'd stay in it. So I said, 'Well, stop beefing about it, and let's go and see that Blue Shadow is decently groomed.'

I stood by while they groomed Blue Shadow, not meaning to do a thing; but their fingers were like bunches of bananas and they made such a mess of the job that I had to give them a hand in the end.

At lunch time they couldn't eat a thing, which didn't please Mummy, and when we went upstairs to dress I had to practically get them into their clothes.

'Do we really look too smart?' said Melly. 'Honestly, I don't want to. Lindo says she's going to wear a bunch of artificial violets on her lapel.'

'If she does,' I said viciously, 'I'll never speak to her again.'

'In books they do,' said Lindo.

'If you want to be laughed at,' I said, 'you're going the right way about it.'

They climbed into their new shirts, fawn breeches, shining boots, black coats, and hard hats. I tied their fawn ties for them.

'Blimey!' I said. 'You're a gift for the photographers.'

Lindo smirked, but Melly looked a bit anxious. She suddenly said, 'I'm not *going* dressed like this. It looks conceited and horrid. Oh, Jill, couldn't you lend me something old?'

I was a bit taken aback and said, 'Gosh, Melly, you wouldn't want to wear my old clothes.'

Melly said, yes she would, and please could she have my jodhs and my tweed jacket with the leather patches on the elbows?

'Of course you can if you want to,' I said; and to make a long story short we hastily bundled Melly out of one lot of clothes and into another, and she looked much better and

more workmanlike, and Lindo looked on superciliously and
said, 'I think you're silly.'

We got to the field in good time. There was a small ring
with benches all round it, and the competitors were waiting
under the trees or giving their ponies practice rides. They
were all local children and a quiet-looking crowd, some of
them obviously inexperienced.

'I don't think much of the opposition,' said Lindo.

'That's the worst mistake you can ever make,' I said, 'to
under-rate the opposition. It leads to some nasty shocks.'

'Oh, Jill, I'm going to die!' said Melly. 'I'm honestly going
to die!'

'Well, don't die when I'm around,' I said brutally, 'because I'm not going to pick up the bits.'

The loud-speaker announced, 'Competitors for Class One
in the ring, please.'

'That's me,' said Lindo, turning pale.

We watched her ride into the ring with about twenty
others, and she certainly looked very striking and rather
like a peacock among a lot of hens. People were saying,
'Who's that marvellous-looking girl on that marvellous
pony?'

'Is she doing all right, Jill?' said Melly anxiously.

'She's holding her reins too tight,' I said, 'and her pony's
overbending. Oh, she is an idiot, she knows not to do that!
Now she's sitting too far forward. She's trying to show off,
why on earth can't she ride naturally?'

Lindo was riding between a tall girl on a long-backed
pony, who sat beautifully and didn't do a thing wrong, and
a fat little boy on a prancing cob which suddenly shot past
Lindo and sent Blue Shadow side-stepping. Lindo lost her
stirrups, bounced in the saddle, and went very red in the
face. By the time they were told to canter she had recovered,

and cantered quite well and on the right leg, which was more than a lot of the competitors did, though she spoilt the effect by constantly pushing her hat back.

Certainly there wasn't a lot of opposition, as some of the competitors looked as though they had only been on a pony about twice before. I placed the fair girl on the long-backed pony first, and a very competent little boy on a well-trained grey second, with Lindo third, and that was how they were actually called in. I felt that Lindo might have been first, and it was all her own fault that she wasn't. Unfortunately, she didn't even keep her third place, as when she was told to unsaddle she began fumbling, and the other children all had their saddles off while Lindo was still pulling helplessly at the buckle.

'It's her own fault,' said Melly. 'She pulled it a hole tighter because she thought it looked smarter, and the hole was new, and now it's stuck.'

Lindo ended up fourth, but there wasn't any Reserve so she was really unplaced and came off looking very dim indeed, with all the bounce taken out of her. Melly grabbed Blue Shadow and began to fuss over her.

'I was just nervous,' Lindo said, 'and I did everything wrong. I wish I could do it again now, and I'd do it right.'

'You must have known,' I said, 'that you were sitting too far forward and pulling the reins.'

'I thought it looked smarter,' said Lindo miserably.

'I saw the judge say something to you,' said Melly. 'What did he say, Lindo?'

'He said, "You've got a beautiful pony there, just try and learn to ride her in a way that's worthy of her." I thought he was a crabby old thing,' said Lindo.

Before anybody could comment on this the loudspeaker announced, 'Competitors for Class Two in the ring, please.'

'Oh, that's me!' gasped Melly. 'Oh, Jill, what shall I do?'

'You're lucky,' said Lindo. 'You've seen how it's done.'

'Keep your head, Melly,' I said. 'And good luck.'

Melly had much harder competition in the senior class, but it was nice to see her let Blue Shadow walk out a little, and then collect her competently. Blue Shadow whisked her tail, looking beautiful and sure of herself. She trotted and cantered, and all the time Melly sat like a ramrod looking straight between her pony's ears. A lot of people met their doom in the canter, what with bucking and crowding and being on the wrong leg, but Melly got round without a mishap.

'She looks as if she was in trance,' said Lindo, giggling.

'She's a bit too stiff,' I said, 'but that isn't counted a bad fault in a competition of this class. Golly!' I yelled. 'She's been called in first!'

It was true. There was Melly starting the winning line, absolutely scarlet in the face, but holding Blue Shadow nicely and keeping very quiet. The others were called in, and you could see that Melly was a bit overcome at having to be the first to lead her pony out in hand, but she didn't make a bad job of it, and when it came to unsaddling she didn't make any mistake, for she had thoughtfully fastened her buckles in well-worn holes the minute she had taken over from Lindo.

Lindo and I stood with our mouths wide open while the judge handed Melly the red rosette, and there was Melly leading the gallop round the field and looking as if she had just come out of a dream.

At that moment I felt almost fond of Melly. We went round to meet her when she came off, and found her sitting on Blue Shadow in the middle of a circle of admiring kids and mothers; at least, one kid was patting Blue Shadow's nose and saying, 'Isn't she gorgeous?' But I heard a mother say that people with professional-looking ponies shouldn't be allowed in children's gymkhanas. Blue Shadow really did look a bit too special for the occasion.

As soon as Melly saw us she stood up in her stirrups and yelled, 'I won! I won! It was dead easy.'

I was so covered with shame that I could have gone through the ground, and far from feeling fond of Melly I could have murdered her.

'Get down, Melly,' I hissed, 'and shut up! Don't swank!'

'I got a red rosette and a pound,' shrieked Melly, bouncing about.

'What did the judge say to you?' said Lindo.

'He said, "Well, you're a big improvement on your sister".'

'I don't believe you,' Lindo exploded. 'You beast!'

'Well, at least,' said Melly, slithering to the ground, 'I'm glad I wore Jill's clothes and wasn't all dolled up like you.'

The next minute these two charming sisters were locked in hand-to-hand combat. It was a disgusting scene. Everybody was watching them, and I couldn't bear it so I walked away, and after a bit they followed me. We ended up at the ice-cream tent where Melly insisted on paying for the ices, which was decent of her, though I still felt mad with her.

'I wish now that we'd entered for a lot more events,' said Lindo. 'I'd like to have another go.'

'I'm jolly glad you didn't,' I said bitterly. 'My nerves wouldn't stand much more of your disgusting manners.'

Melly gave an imitation of a pricked balloon, and said sulkily, 'Well, I couldn't help being excited. Anyway, I've paid for the ices.'

'Don't rub it in,' I said coldly.

We came out of the tent, and I said, 'By the way, where's Blue Shadow?'

'Oh, murder!' said Melly. 'I just left her.'

You mean, you just *left* her?' said Lindo. 'Well, of all the *dopes*!'

We started to run to where Melly had left Blue Shadow, and there she was in the middle of a crowd of small kids who were giving each other rides on her, which wasn't doing her any good at all. Melly drove them off and caught hold of Blue Shadow who was by now thoroughly frightened, tossing her head and shivering. She nearly had Melly off her feet, and in the end I had to take her bridle and soothe her down. I led her off into the shade of the trees, rubbed her down, and gave her some oats, talking to her gently. Melly and Lindo were both a bit subdued by now, and on the way home Melly said, 'I'm sorry I made an idiot of myself. But I couldn't help being excited.'

'That's okay, Melly,' I said. 'You won't do it again. You've just got to learn to be frightfully good-mannered at a gymkhana whether you win or lose.'

'Well, I lost,' said Lindo, 'and I didn't behave too badly, except that if I hadn't tried to show off I would probably have won. I expect showing off is bad manners too.'

'Oh!' yelled Melly in an agonized way. 'I've lost my red rosette! Oh, how awful!'

'It's okay,' said Lindo in a rather shamed kind of voice. 'It's in my pocket. I grabbed it when we were fighting, and I was going to throw it away just to spite you for calling me dolled up, but I'm sorry. Here it is.'

'Well, you two!' I said.

Then they both had a bit of a weep, but I got them mopped up before we reached home. Mummy was at the gate, waving.

'Hullo!' she said. 'Tell me what happened. I can't wait.'

'Quite good,' I said. 'Melly won her class – look at Blue Shadow with her rosette! – and Lindo was fourth, only there wasn't a reserve prize or she'd have had it.'

Mummy said, that was wonderful, and she knew something nice would happen so she'd got us a special supper. After supper I went out to feed my ponies, and Melly and Lindo came after me and said they thought I'd been decent and they felt a bit wormlike.

'The ices were thirty pence,' said Melly, 'so there's seventy pence left out of the pound, and I'd like you to have it, Jill, to buy something for your stable.'

'Oh, don't be silly,' I said. 'Forget it, Melly.'

'You won't refuse to take us to any more Shows, will you?' said Lindo, and I felt very embarrassed and said that we all made mistakes; and Lindo said, was all forgiven and forgotten? and I said, of course it was and don't be so idiotic in future, and Melly said, she'd clean my tack for me tomorrow as a sort of penance. And actually she did.

13

Nobody was watching me

MUMMY said how nice it was to see me getting on so well with Melly and Lindo, and what fun that they shared all my interests, and I just said nothing. For one thing, I felt she might have noticed for herself that I was practically wilting away from having to cope with the Cortmans; and for another, there isn't any point in arguing with grown-ups because they just can't see your point of view. Then Mummy was very biased towards the Cortmans, partly because of their being the daughters of her dearest friend, and partly because in their infancy they had read all her children's books and thought them whizzo. Also Mrs Crosby, our daily help, was biased towards them because they always remembered every morning to ask her about her rheumatism, which I never did. So you can see that if I had complained that Melly and Lindo gave me a pain in the neck I shouldn't have got any sympathy.

They were now learning to jump, and we got nothing but jumping talk from morning till night. Of course there is nothing I like more than talking about jumping, but to hear Lindo drooling on with excitement for hours because she had jumped two-foot six – *and* on a trained show jumper – was more than I could stand.

Melly said, 'Do come up to Mrs Darcy's and see us jump, Jill.'

'Yes, do go, Jill,' said Mummy. 'The girls want to show you how well they're getting on.'

Melly and Lindo were certainly being very well taught by Mrs Darcy, and they were whales for lessons, always wanting more and more and more; but the pleasure to me lay in watching the action of Blue Shadow who certainly was a dream of a jumper.

'What did you think of us?' said Melly, when they had each done a round of the nursery jumps. I had to admit that they weren't doing badly at all.

'Mrs Darcy says that I may be good enough to ride in the junior jumping at Chatton Show,' said Lindo with great satisfaction. 'It's hard luck on Melly being fifteen, because she won't be good enough for the senior class. I shall be competing against you and all your friends, Jill.'

Without being disloyal to my ponies I could not help gazing longingly at Blue Shadow, with her beautiful arched neck and her thin elegant legs.

'Would you like a go on her?' said Melly in a sudden burst of generosity.

'Oh, could I?' I said, brightening up.

I certainly didn't wait for the invitation to be withdrawn. It was lovely on Blue Shadow's back, feeling her effortless canter and the sure competence with which she approached each jump. She needed very little aid from me, and we seemed to flow over the jumps.

Mrs Darcy came out and said, 'She needs something more than a nursery course, Jill. Take her into the big field.'

'Oh, can I?' I said to Melly.

Melly said I could, and Lindo said, 'Well, don't lame her or anything.' I could have retorted that if anybody was likely to lame Blue Shadow it would be Lindo in one of her showing-off moods, but I meekly said nothing.

I felt a bit nervous, but I did two easy three-foot jumps, then a four-foot, and finally the tricky four-foot six, when we brought down the top bar. I think that was my fault, because I had checked Blue Shadow when I need not, for she had the situation well in hand.

I brought her in and said to Mrs Darcy, 'I should think she's a gift in any competition. I don't see how she could lose.'

'I'm not so sure about that,' said Mrs Darcy. 'She's marvellous on her own, but she isn't so good with other horses. She seems to be conscious that she's competing and gets over-excited. I had her round the jumps the other night with Pansy and Pat, and she was watching their ponies when she ought to have been looking at nothing but the course. I had to hold her very hard. She's by no means a ride for anybody inexperienced.'

'Oh, help!' yelled Lindo. 'What about me in the under-fourteens?'

'Oh, you needn't worry. You'll be perfectly all right in a juvenile class, because Blue Shadow can take those jumps and think of something else at the same time, which is more than any pony can do when she's on a tricky jumping course. Her fault is that she's easily distracted.'

'She's divine to ride,' I sighed, smoothing the back of my hand over Blue Shadow's satin shoulder.

'What a pity you haven't a better pony, Jill,' said Melly, 'because then you'd be able to win a lot of competitions. You don't ride too badly at all.'

I was so dumbfounded by these appalling remarks that for about ten seconds I was speechless. Then I came round, and I went for Melly tooth and nail, but I knew that I wasn't doing myself any good. We were back where we started at the beginning of this story. I hadn't done a single thing to impress these frightful girls, and they still thought

I was no good at all. I felt so low, mere, wormish, and miserable that I could have howled.

When I poured all this out to my friend Ann Derry that night she merely laughed heartlessly, and asked, what did it matter what the Cortmans thought, anyway? They wouldn't be here for long. I said I didn't care if they were only here for five minutes, I had got to do something to impress them because if I didn't I should lose my nerve and have to retire from the world of equitation; and Ann said, 'Well, if you feel like that, why don't you enter for the Fentham Hall fête next week, and take them with you?'

'But it's such a potty little one-eyed affair,' I said.

'Melly and Lindo won't know that, and with your experience you're sure to pick up about four prizes.'

'Humph!' I said.

The Fentham Hall fête was got up every year by a woman called Mrs Leevers, and she used to come round on a bicycle asking us all to enter for the gymkhana, 'because it's such fun and encourages the little ones,' and we used to spend most of our time trying to think of excuses for getting out of it. I do not want to suggest that we were snooty, or thought an awful lot of ourselves, or were against encouraging the young entry, but there are some things in the world of equitation which flesh and blood cannot stand, and the Fentham Hall fête was one of them. One reason was that Mrs Leevers herself insisted on being one of the judges, though she knew as much about riding as a sheep; but it was her fête so naturally nobody could object or say, Not likely!

'Oh, all right,' I said. 'But you'll have to come too. If you can bear it, I can.'

When Melly and Lindo heard that we were all going to the fête they were wildly excited, and decided that they were going to enter Blue Shadow for everything and ride her in turns.

'You can't do that,' I said, horrified. 'You'll tire her out; and besides, a pony of that quality oughtn't to be ridden in free-for-all competitions like Musical Mats and Potato Races. Apart from anything else, she'd probably get kicked.'

'What about Black Boy?' said Lindo. 'Won't he get kicked?'

'No,' I said, 'he won't. Because I'm too clever to let him get kicked. After all, I have had a little more experience than you.'

'Really?' said Lindo sarkily. 'I can't say I'd noticed it.'

I am happy to tell you that I was noble enough not to punch Lindo on the nose. With a wisdom beyond my years I realized that it was no use beefing about what I could do until I had actually shown it.

We set off for Fentham Hall the following Saturday afternoon, on a grey and windy day. Melly and Lindo tossed up as to which was to ride Blue Shadow and which was to ride the bike, and Melly won. Lindo said she had meant the best out of three, and Melly said she wasn't playing that game any more, she'd won the toss and she was sticking to it. Ann met us at the gates, on her pony George, and said, 'Come on, you three. We'd better go and do our entries for the gymkhana at once, and get our numbers.' But Melly and Lindo were looking at the side-shows spread out under the trees, and said, 'Oh, there's no hurry, can't we do some of these competitions first?'

Ann grumbled that we didn't want to have to stand in a queue for half an hour to enter for the gymkhana; and Lindo said maddeningly, 'Oh, there won't be all that much rush. Let's go and do that thing where you throw rings over prizes. Melly's a whizz at that game, aren't you, Melly?'

Rather reluctantly we tied our ponies to the adjacent

fence, and went over to the stall. You got three rings for
five pence, so we paid and I had the first go. It was very
difficult. The rings bounced off the board, or knocked the
prizes over, and I had no luck. Then Lindo tried and was no
better than me. When it was Ann's turn she nearly got a
bottle of tomato sauce, but though the ring fell over it the
bottle went down, and the woman at the stall said it didn't
count. Then it was Melly's turn.

'Watch this,' said Lindo.

With Melly's first throw she got a tin of cocoa; with her
second throw she got a mending set with needles and
things; with her third throw she got a pink plush teddy bear.

'Oh, go on, let's have another bash,' said Lindo. 'It's only
five pence.'

The woman at the stall who was in a pink dress and a
floral hat didn't look too pleased, and looked very dim,
indeed, when Melly's second attempt landed a packet of fruit
pastilles, a pen-and-pencil set, and a voucher for a free tea.
Ann, Lindo and I again got nothing.

'Go it, Melly!' said Lindo. 'You're right on form.'

I said I thought Melly ought to stop, as it was rather awful
to take so many prizes; but Melly said, Bosh! The prizes
were there to be won, and if people didn't want them to be
won they shouldn't put them on the stall; and I said, yes,
but people didn't expect anybody to get six prizes for ten
pence; and Melly said that actually it was forty pence because Lindo and Ann and I had paid ten pence each without
winning anything; and I said, 'Oh, I can't argue for ever,
come *on*!' And Melly said, no, she was going to stay and
have another try.

Ann said, 'Well, Jill and I are going to enter for the
gymkhana, so you'd better hurry after us, or you'll be left
out.'

Ann and I untied our ponies and led them over to where it said GYMKHANA THIS WAY. We entered for a lot of events and got our numbers, and then I said, 'Melly and Lindo haven't turned up. They are crazy. Do you think we ought to go and find them?'

'I shouldn't bother,' said Ann. 'They're old enough to find their own way, and if they don't it's their loss.'

'Well, they're missing the showing class,' I said, 'because it's being called in now.'

I must admit that it wasn't a very good gymkhana or one that Ann and I would have entered for in the ordinary course of events, as quite a lot of the children in it had never been in a competition before, and quite a lot of the ponies hadn't the vaguest idea what it was all about. I won the showing class, and Ann was second. We then went into the senior showing class, which was a bit better standard, and Ann won it and I was second. There was no sign of Melly and Lindo, which seemed a bit ironical as I was only doing this to impress them.

'I must go and look for them,' I said. 'I'm supposed to be in charge of them, and Mummy would be mad if she knew I'd let them wander loose.'

Ann said, Well, should we just do the Musical Poles first? I said, all right; so I won the Musical Poles – it was the sort of day when I couldn't do anything wrong – and then we went to look for Melly and Lindo, but there were about a thousand people milling about in the grounds and they weren't to be seen at any of the side-shows; so Ann and I went back to the gymkhana and I won the Bending Race and Ann was second.

'Don't you think we'd better ease off?' said Ann. 'I mean, we're as bad as Melly, winning all these prizes.'

So we went to look for Melly and Lindo again, but we

didn't find them. The reason we didn't find them was that they were changing their clothes in a luxurious bedroom upstairs in Fentham Hall, and afterwards being served with a luxurious tea in the luxurious drawing-room of that same ancestral pile. This was, as we eventually learned, because they were heroes. After they had finished throwing rings, they had wandered along to have a look at the lake which was glimmering through the trees, and on which a small boy called Ernest Postlethwaite was sailing on a raft of his own construction. The raft capsized and Ernest Postlethwaite went into about ten feet of water and yelled, Help! A lot of people came running when Ernest yelled Help! but nobody did anything except Lindo, who threw off her coat and dived in and swam to Ernest and life-saved him out very efficiently. Ernest by then was full of water and looked rather dead, so Melly took him over and laid him on his tummy and artificially respirated him until he came round, in the presence of quite a crowd. Everybody said that Melly and Lindo were marvellous, and what presence of mind! Lindo said it was nothing, just a piece of cake, and they did Life-saving Practice at their school swimming pool every week, and Melly and she had got a medal for it at the school sports, and they'd always wanted to do a real rescue but had never had the chance until now; and it was a pity that Ernest Postlethwaite had come round so quickly, because Melly was just getting into her stride and would have liked him to be deader than he actually was.

By now Mrs Leevers who owned Fentham Hall had turned up, and she said that Melly and Lindo were heroes and must go straight back to the Hall with her and change into dry clothes and have some nice hot tea; which they didn't object to at all.

Meanwhile, Ann and I had done the Jumping Competition

with clear rounds, and had jumped off with two other people, and been bracketed first, so we rode out with our ponies' browbands stiff with rosettes, and went to look for Melly and Lindo again, but all we found was Blue Shadow still tied to the fence by the entrance and looking very bored and sorry for herself.

'Good gracious!' I gasped. 'Where on earth can they have gone to?'

Ann said that she didn't see why worrying about Melly and Lindo should spoil our afternoon when what we really needed was tea and ices; so we went and had these, but I couldn't help worrying and wondering what Mummy would say to me for not sticking to the Cortmans.

The tea marquee was near the main entrance to the Hall, and as we came out Ann gasped and said, 'Who's that – coming down the steps – with Mrs Leevers? It *can't* be –'

Mrs Leevers had a girl on each side of her, and those girls looked awfully like Melly and Lindo, except that one of them had on a pink linen dress that was too big for her, and the other one had on a white dress with blue flowers that was too big for her, and the last time we had seen Melly and Lindo they had been wearing their riding clothes.

'But it is!' I said. 'Whatever's happened?'

'Oh, those are the frightfully brave girls that rescued the little boy from the lake,' said a woman who was standing next to us.

'Gosh!' I said.

Lindo then caught sight of me and said, 'Hullo, Jill!' and I went over, and Mrs Leevers said, 'You ought to be very proud of your friends.'

In the end, Melly and Lindo, clutching a two-pound box of chocolates which Mrs Leevers had given them, were driven home — leaving their wet clothes behind to be dried — in Mrs Leevers' opulent limousine, while Ann and I rode back, she on George and leading Black Boy and Blue Shadow, and I on the bike, feeling a bit *infra dig*, in spite of all those rosettes.

'Isn't this just Life?' I said bitterly. 'I go to all the trouble of entering for this mere and wormish gymkhana, and riding in all these events, and I win all these rosettes just to impress Melly and Lindo; and nobody could care less, because Melly and Lindo have got to go and be heroes the minute my back's turned, and get all that glory and all those chocolates!'

Ann did nothing but giggle. She said she was sorry for me, and it certainly was just like Life, but it was also too funny for words.

By the time I got home, Melly and Lindo had changed into their own skirts and blouses, and Mummy had given them hot lemon and an aspirin in case they had caught cold, and was saying, 'Now what did really happen?' and Melly said modestly, 'It wasn't anything; in fact, we enjoyed it,' and Lindo insisted on me having half the chocolates.

Nobody even remembered the gymkhana, or noticed that Black Boy was practically smothered in red and blue rosettes, so I just took them off and threw them in a drawer with the others and gave a hollow laugh, like they do in books. It seemed to me that the noble cause of equitation had taken rather a back seat; but Black Boy had been marvellous, and I told him so as I rubbed him down and fed him. I have noticed that however peculiarly human beings behave the ponies always do their part bravely and without any fuss, and this is why the horse is acknowledged to be the most noble animal in the world.

14
How we practised

I HOPE I have not given the impression that I spent the whole time running around and getting into scrapes in order to show Melly and Lindo what a fine rider I was, because such was not the case. Nor was I neglecting my own ponies to gaze in sickening admiration at Blue Shadow. I was thinking very hard about Chatton Show and my ambition to win one of the juvenile events there.

My friend Ann Derry and I had laboriously made for ourselves an adequate jumping course in the paddock behind Ann's house. I say laboriously, because nobody had offered to buy us any wonderful-looking professional-type gates and bars or wood blocks for walls, no wings or white paint or anything like that. We had to invent and discover everything for ourselves, and it had taken us *years*; during which time we had prowled round the district with greedy eyes, looking for things that people didn't want and which would do for our jumps. We didn't actually use old iron bedsteads, as some children in books are supposed to do, because though other children's ponies may like jumping over iron bedsteads Ann and I were sure that ours would only break their knees. We just hung round farms, and even did odd jobs, and collected a crumbly sort of gate and some poles, and we made a wall out of cartons from the grocer's – only it got a bit soggy in wet weather; and the crowning thing was that when the new gym was built at our school and refurnished, we managed to buy the old jumping stand for fifty pence, complete with pegs. This happened in the winter when we hadn't any prize money behind us, and were consequently completely broke, and had to save all our pocket money and go without sweets. However, it was worth it.

We stored all the stuff as we got it, in Ann's greenhouse, and there was a weekly row about this when Ann's mother went to water the cacti, but we survived and so did the stuff. Ann's birthday came in May, and she asked her mother for white and red paint for a present, which I thought was frightfully noble of her when I knew how much she wanted a bedside lamp with a clock in it. Ann's mother just said, 'I think you're quite mad,' and kindly ordered the tins of paint; and as I managed to win a small competition about that time I spent the prize money on two brushes.

So we had our jumps in time for the summer, and we spent hours and hours of work on them, and they looked lovely and fell down very easily, which was really an asset. The jumping stand from the gym proved a big success, as Ann's father who was in a mellow mood had some long steel pegs made for us at his factory, to support a good-sized pole; and we filled in the front with a piece of garden trellis which had once supported some rambler roses at the vicarage, until it rotted at the bottom and fell down, and the vicar's wife was delighted when we offered to take it away.

Though everything looked rather scruffy and odd before it was finished, by the time we had had a few sessions with the tins of red and white paint the whole set-up looked so professional that we nearly swooned. We could only stand gazing in admiration, hardly able to believe that this was our jumping course, created by our brilliant brains and the sweat of our brows, as Shakespeare says. Ann, who was getting rather businesslike, suggested that we might have an opening and ask all our friends round to try our jumps for five pence, which would help the funds; but we didn't do that, because I said that they would probably do a great deal more than five pence-worth each of damage.

People at school were very interested, and somebody – I think it was Susan Pyke – said to Ann, 'I hear you've got a round of jumps made entirely out of cardboard?' Ann said, 'Yes, isn't it wonderful, we've discovered that cardboard is just as jumpable as anything else,' which squashed Susan Pyke.

We began to use the jumps at once, and found them a marvellous help, especially the jumping-stand. We had made up our minds to take first and second places in the fourteen-and-under at Chatton, and I had giddy visions of being a success also in the under-sixteens. I had nothing to lose, and Rapide was becoming a cunning and competent jumper and loved the game. I never had to encourage him to jump; it was his favourite occupation, and my trouble at shows was to keep him from whinnying with delight at the sight of the jumps and thus making my face go red with shame. I mean, it is frightful to ride a pony round a jumping course when it is yelling with joy all the time. This happened to me once, and the judges thought I was trying to be funny and the crowd thought the pony was in pain, so I was very unpopular all round.

Ann and I were happy because our ponies took to our jumps at once and approved of them, and didn't complain because they were made of bits and pieces. Actually, cardboard or not, we considered them highly scientific jumps, and we had spent ages in adjusting the heights and the distances apart and the angles of approach.

Ann said, 'Rapide jumps like a stag,' and I sighed and

said that I wished he was half as graceful as a stag, and she ought to see Blue Shadow jump. Ann said it was all right seeing Blue Shadow jump, except that one's mind was distracted by the appalling bouncing of her rider, whether it was Melly or Lindo, and any horse that could be graceful under such circumstances ought to have a medal for endurance.

I giggled a bit over this, and then shut up, remembering that it is both silly and rude to under-rate other people, so I said, 'We'd better not be so jolly superior about Melly and Lindo. Mrs Darcy is training them and she won't let them go on bouncing. They may get frightfully good and beat us yet.'

When the schedules were out for Chatton Show we became very excited. Ann got ours, and brought it round to the cottage, and we spread it out on the kitchen table, and I found some apples to fortify us while we were reading.

Ann said, 'Well, the only classes which concern us are the two juvenile showing classes, and the two juvenile jumping classes, so that settles that. Gosh, what a lot of classes there are! There's a silver bowl for the under-sixteen showing class.'

'Bags I that for Black Boy,' I said.

Ann said, 'You've a hope! And there's a silver cup for the under-sixteen jumping, but you needn't say "Bags I that for Rapide" because you'll be lucky if you get out with less than six faults.'

'I don't care,' I said. 'It's going to be fun.'

We carefully did our entries, and went down to the Post Office and got the postal orders and sent them off, and when I got home I took the schedule up to my room and looked at it again. It was rather interesting because it said that there would be a special juvenile competition for a three-minute display of horsemanship.

A big noise suddenly broke out downstairs. It was Melly and Lindo, and they started shouting, 'Jill! Jill! We've got the schedule for Chatton Show and Mrs Darcy says —'

So I went down, and found them very excited because Mrs Darcy had said there was no reason why Melly shouldn't show Blue Shadow in the under-sixteen showing class, and Lindo ride her in a jumping class.

'Isn't it marvellous?' said Lindo. 'Of course we've both come on a lot since you watched us, and Mrs Darcy says that even if I get twelve faults she's seen some of the best riders do the same.'

'I wish I was good enough to do it,' said Melly. 'I don't see why Lindo should be better than me.'

I replied rather absent-mindedly, because I was thinking about this individual show. It would have to be something special, and I made up my mind that I would work out a little programme for Black Boy and teach him to do it if it took me all day every day until the Show. He was a good and patient learner, and I was ambitious. I decided I would try to do a collected walk, some half-passes, and finally a collected canter changing legs every four steps. It sounds simple, and it would look simple, but if it was perfectly done it would be impressive. I couldn't wait to try it, but needless to say, when it came to actual practice I found I had taken on quite a lot.

I told Mrs Darcy what I was doing, and she said it was quite a good programme if it didn't come unstuck.

'Unstuck is the word,' I said. 'At present I'm getting him to change legs every eight steps, only usually it's either seven or nine or six. I work on it for hours until we're both fed up.'

'Whatever you do you mustn't let Black Boy get bored,' said Mrs Darcy. 'Loosen him up with a ride on the Common and then give him an hour's steady schooling and make it plain what you want him to do.'

'Oh, I do,' I said. 'Then he gets a reward of an apple, and we have another session.'

Mrs Darcy said, why didn't I ask Mr Prescott to give me some hints? and I said, 'Oh, do you think I could?'

I didn't think there was any harm in trying, so I wrote to Mr Prescott and told him what I was trying to do, and he promised to come over and see us all at work. Melly and Lindo couldn't wait to show him how well they were riding and jumping Blue Shadow.

'Lindo has come on very well in a very short time,' said Mr Prescott to me.

I said, 'Well, I think the reason is that she's absolutely fearless. It never seems to occur to her that there's any reason why she shouldn't jump a four-foot wall. She leaves it all to Blue Shadow. But Mrs Darcy says that Blue Shadow isn't so good in competition because she gets over-excited when she sees other ponies, and Lindo isn't experienced enough to cope with that.'

'I suppose you're hoping to pick up a few prizes yourself at Chatton,' said Mr Prescott; and I replied, not very modestly, that I would be satisfied with winning one juvenile jumping class, but my heart was set on winning the competition with the individual programme.

'Let's have a look at Black Boy, then,' said Mr Prescott.

We worked for an hour and he helped me tremendously. 'It's just a matter of skill and control,' he said. 'Above all, take it very slowly and calmly. I wish I could show you, but if I mounted Black Boy my feet would touch the ground and he'd cockle up. Let's try again.'

'I wish I knew what other people are doing,' I said.

'Perhaps they're all practising marvellous circus tricks and my programme will look just silly.'

'Pooh!' said Mr Prescott. 'Believe me, the judges don't want to see circus tricks. Skill and control, as I said before. That's what the judges want to see. Come on, Jill. You're getting fours now.'

'More likely fives and threes,' I said despondently. 'But the half passes seem to be coming right, thank goodness.'

For the next three weeks we all lived and ate and dreamed Chatton Show. My job was to keep what I was doing with Black Boy a grim secret from my friends, and as the time drew nearer and Black Boy got better and better, it was very hard to find a time for practising when I would not be surrounded by interested faces. In the end I found the only thing to do was to drag myself out of bed an hour earlier in the mornings, eat and then dash out for a long, peaceful practice. I was safe then, because Melly and Lindo didn't come round to the cottage before eight-thirty or nine, and I knew that however curious my friends – such as Ann and Diana – were, they certainly weren't energetic enough to appear before breakfast. Black Boy was doing his programme so well now that I was almost frightened. It was still a week before the Show, and I didn't want him to reach his best too soon and then begin to go stale. I even used to worry about this in bed at night, and I wondered if, like people in books, I should wake up in the morning to find that my hair had turned white; in fact, as dawn broke I would shoot out of bed and rush straight to the looking-glass to get reassured and then drag on a sweater and jodhs and rush out to my little paddock to share with Black Boy the delights of sniffing the early dew.

In the afternoons we would all go to the jumping course at Ann's place, and jump each other's ponies for variety of practice, and I must say that Melly and Lindo were very decent about letting me jump Blue Shadow; though when it was a case of a ride on the Common I always let one of them ride Black Boy.

The day but one before the Show I thought I had better go and get my hair cut, because I thought it would make me look neater and more experienced than to appear with a mop of blowing locks. Mummy gave me the money and said, 'Run along to Mrs Parson's' – which was the village hairdresser's – but I had other ideas. I had seen some pictures of nifty hair styles in a magazine of Mummy's, they were beautifully jagged and Italian-looking, and I decided I would go into Ryechester to a very splendid establishment called Maison Chic, and pay the difference out of my hard-earned pocket money.

I came back on the five o'clock bus feeling very well satisfied, and Mummy said, 'Gosh, you do look sophisticated! Mrs Parsons must have bucked up her ideas a bit.'

I told her I had been to Maison Chic and felt very Italian and pleased with myself, and I spent most of tea-time standing in front of the looking-glass with a buttered bun in my hand, and Lindo said, 'Swank!' and Melly said the effect would be lost at the Show as I'd have to ride in a hat.

While we were having tea it began to rain hard, so I said I'd better go and take the ponies in and feed them.

Melly said, 'Oh, that's all right, Jill. We've done it for you.'

'Are you quite well?' I said.

'We had Black Boy out for a ride,' said Lindo. 'We forgot to ask you before you went, but we knew you wouldn't mind, so when we came back we thought we'd stable both the ponies for you.'

'Thanks,' I said. 'Actually, I'd rather that Black Boy

wasn't ridden by anybody but me as it's so near to the Show, but I don't suppose it's done him any harm.'

I thought Melly had rather an odd expression on her face, but nobody said anything, and when I went out to the stable to say good night to the ponies they were both quiet and contented, Rapide standing with a sly smirk on his face and Black Boy lying on his straw and whinnying with pleasure when he saw me.

Next morning I got up early as usual, and whistled as I leapt into my old grey sweater and my jodhs, and tossed my Italian locks. It was a beautiful sunny morning and the air smelt delicious when I unlocked the back door and slipped out into the yard.

I unlocked the stable door and went in. Rapide gave the little jump he always did when I appeared, restless to get out; but to my surprise Black Boy was still lying down as though he hadn't moved from the night before.

'Come on, Boy – up!' I said, taking him by the halter, but he didn't attempt to get up. I encouraged him, and heaved, and suddenly he stood up as though trying to oblige me.

'Come on, lazy,' I said, and began to lead him out. Then I saw to my horror that he was dragging his off-hind foot. I stopped and felt it, and it was horribly hot and limp. I was so stunned by this awful and unexpected disaster that I couldn't believe it. I told myself, it can't be much, he'll be all right when he gets outside; but by now Black Boy was standing still and shivering in a miserable sort of way, and wouldn't move at all. He turned his head and looked at me as if to say, Oh, dear, what has happened to me? His usually bright eyes were dull, and his ears drooped and his coat was damp with sweat.

'Oh, gosh!' I said. 'Oh, darling, Black Boy, what have you done?'

I sat down on the stable floor and took his bad foot on my knee, trying to tell myself that a bit of stroking would put it right, but I knew I should have to get the vet. Even then I hoped that he would have some magic way of making the foot right in a few minutes.

Rapide started making a noise as much as to say he wanted his breakfast, and what was all this fuss over Black Boy, anyway?

I did the feeds. Black Boy wouldn't eat a thing, so I turned Rapide into the orchard and went back to my poor pony.

15
My poor, poor pony

SOON there was a patter of feet and some excited barks, and the two dogs of the Cortmans came rushing to find me, as they usually did when fetched from their kennels. Melly and Lindo were in my midst.

'What's the matter?' said Melly when she saw me sitting on the floor.

'It's Black Boy's foot,' I said. 'Look at the swelling. I'm just going to ring the vet.'

Melly went pink and said, 'What's the matter with it?' Lindo said, 'I don't suppose there's much wrong.'

Suddenly I remembered in a flash that she and Melly had had Black Boy out yesterday afternoon while I was at the hairdesser's.

'What have you done to him?' I said furiously.

Lindo said feebly, 'It wasn't anything really. I didn't know he was hurt. We got a bit mixed up with a car.'

'You did what?' I yelled. 'You don't mean to say you took Black Boy on the main road!'

'Well, we wanted to go to Moss Lane, and –'

'You absolute idiot!' I said. 'And why on earth didn't you tell me last night?'

'Honestly, Jill,' said Melly, 'we didn't know there was anything wrong. He just limped a bit, but he seemed all right.'

I jumped up.

'I'll never forgive you as long as I live,' I said. 'Get out of my way! I'm going to ring the vet.'

I managed to catch the vet before he set off on his morning round, and he arrived within half an hour.

'Nasty sprain,' he said. 'But I can't tell if there's a fracture until I get the swelling reduced. What happened?'

I gritted my teeth, and said, 'Apparently a car touched him.'

'Oh? That's unfortunate. Well, we'll have him all right in a week if there's no fracture.'

'A week?' I shrieked. 'It's Chatton Show on Saturday.'

The vet whistled. 'Oh, rough luck. Were you going to show him? Well, I'm afraid that's all washed up.'

The vet bandaged the leg and gave me a lot of instructions. Then he went away. Melly and Lindo were hanging about outside the stable.

'What did he say?' said Lindo. 'Will it be all right for Saturday?'

I simply blazed. 'No, it won't,' I said. 'It's going to be at least a week, and I've spent ages training him for the individual display competition, and he was perfect, and now it's all no use. You two are not only idiots, you're foul, and I loathe you. I've loathed you from the very minute you came here.'

'We're terribly sorry,' said Melly.

'Yes, we are,' said Lindo. 'We really are, Jill.'

'Oh, shut up,' I said, and rushed into the cottage. I was so blind with rage and misery that I bumped full tilt into Mummy and nearly knocked her flat. She said, 'What *are* you doing? You might be more careful, Jill.'

I said, 'Ask Lindo if you want to know,' and tore up to my room and slammed the door. Then I began to cry like mad, which was thing I hadn't done since I was about ten.

About five minutes later Mummy came in and said, 'You mustn't go on like this, Jill. It doesn't do any good.'

I blew my nose furiously and said, 'I'm all right now. Nothing's any good, anyway. Only keep those two away from me or I'll chop them into little pieces.'

'Oh, Jill!' said Mummy sorrowfully, and put her arm round me and patted the bit of me that was nearest. 'It is a shame, and the hardest luck after all the work you've put in. But it was an accident, you know, and accidents can happen anywhere at any minute, to any pony or any person.'

'In the first place,' I blazed, 'they'd no business to take Black Boy out without asking me. And I'd told them a million times that they must *never* go on the main road, because they're completely inexperienced with ponies in traffic. And they do it, and *their* pony gets away with it, and *my* pony gets ruined! And then they didn't even tell me last night, when I might have been able to do something for that foot!'

'They didn't think there was anything wrong,' said Mummy. 'They're both frightfully sorry and crying their eyes out.'

'I'm jolly glad to hear it,' I said. 'And I hope their beastly eyes stop out and never go in again.'

'Well, what are we going to do?' said Mummy. 'We've just got to accept it, haven't we? And you'll have to make the best of jumping Rapide. I'm sure you're going to be a sensible girl over this.'

'Oh, yes, I'll be sensible,' I said, 'and I'll jump Rapide; only, Mummy, *please* send these horrible Cortmans away — now, today! Please, please, Mummy!'

'But I've nowhere to send them,' she said. 'They've nowhere to go. And I should feel so dreadfully mean. Of course they did wrong, but they didn't do it on purpose, and they're so upset and miserable. You know I'm fairly wise, don't you?'

'Yes,' I grunted.

'Then you must believe me when I say that the right thing to do is to say, "It's all over now," and make the best of things, and I'll take you all into Ryechester for lunch and the pictures.'

'You can take *them*,' I said. 'I'm not going.'

I admit I was now behaving very badly indeed, and upsetting Mummy which I had no right to do.

'Okay,' she said quietly. 'Then do you want your lunch brought up here, or are you coming down for it?'

I gave a big sigh. 'I'll come down,' I said. 'But I won't forgive them!'

As soon as Mummy had left me I rushed off to Mrs Darcy's and poured out the whole awful story.

'Jolly hard luck,' she said. 'I know what it's like. Once I was going to jump at Wembley and I had a most beautiful mare, and another girl took her out for some exercise the afternoon before, and lamed her.'

'Gosh!' I said. 'What did you do?'

'Well, what could I do? The poor kid was in floods of tears, and it was an accident, and it taught her a lesson for life. You've got to accept these things, Jill. Buck up! Just make up your mind you're going to win the under-fourteen jumping on Rapide. I think you probably will.'

'I bet Lindo does,' I said miserably. 'Blue Shadow's so marvellous.'

'If you let Lindo beat you,' said Mrs Darcy in a very spirited voice, 'I'll never speak to you again.'

'Right!' I said. 'I won't let her beat me.'

'That's more like you, Jill,' said Mrs Darcy. 'But take my advice and make it up with Lindo and Melly before the

Show, *because riding in a bad mood is the surest way I know of getting twenty-four faults.* If you're angry and miserable your pony is nervous and depressed. It wouldn't be fair to a nice pony like Rapide to do a thing like that to him, when he's ready to do his best for you.'

I could see this was right, but I didn't know how it was all going to work out. I walked home very slowly, and when I got half-way along the lane, to my horror I saw Melly and Lindo coming towards me.

Melly said, 'We were looking out for you.'

'Okay,' I said. 'It's all finished and I'm not going to talk about it any more. I don't forgive you, but I'm going to be decent to you because Mummy and Mrs Darcy want me to, and for no other reasons.'

Lindo said, 'But that's not all, Jill. We've thought of something. We're so terribly sorry, and we've been talking about what we could do to show we're not beasts. And we've decided that we want you to ride Blue Shadow for us in *both* the juvenile jumping events on Saturday.'

'What?' I said. 'Have you gone mad, or have I?'

'We mean it,' said Melly. 'And we've already sent off the entry to be altered. We want it to say, "Blue Shadow, owned by the Misses Cortman, ridden by Jill Crewe," like they have it at Wembley. Oh, Jill, you will, won't you? You've ridden Blue Shadow so often, and you can have a long practice on her this afternoon. We told your mother what we wanted to do, and she said she thought it was a marvellous idea.'

'Oh, please say yes, Jill,' said Lindo. 'Melly and I will each ride her in a showing class, and you'll ride her in both the jumping classes, and we'll watch you from the rails, and I know you'll win.'

'But – but – but –' I said.

Lindo began to cry. As I have said before, she often did.

'We're not really beasts,' she sobbed. 'Honestly, we're not. And if you ride Blue Shadow and win we'll be happier than if we'd done it ourselves.'

'And Rapide,' I said. 'I'd be riding two horses in each event.'

'Oh, yes,' said Melly. 'It would be wonderful. And I know you'd win, and then perhaps you'd like us a little bit.'

I was stunned. I said, 'It's awfully decent of you. I can't believe it. I don't know whether I ought to. But if Mummy and Mrs Darcy say it's all right –'

'Of course it's all right,' said Lindo. 'Because Melly and I haven't a chance to win in the jumping, and we'd only look as if we were showing off, and we've decided that we're jolly well not going to show off any more.'

'I say, it is decent of you,' I said. 'And as for showing off, I think I've done more of it than you have. Look, Lindo, do stop crying. I've been a beast too. We've all been beasts, so let's shut up about Black Boy, and I do forgive you, and I'm sorry I said I loathed you. Could we go now and ask Mrs Darcy what she thinks?'

'That's all right,' said Melly. 'We telephoned her about a quarter of an hour ago, and she said she thought it was very sporting of us' – she blushed modestly – 'and that we wouldn't be any good at jumping anyway, and we were very sensible to give Blue Shadow a chance with you to ride her. So that's all settled.'

'Gosh, you do think of things!' I said. 'I say, I'm jolly hungry.'

'That's okay, too,' said Lindo. 'We've brought you a choc ice.'

When Mummy saw us all come home together eating choc ices she knew everything was all right, and she looked terribly happy.

'What would you like best for lunch, if you could choose?' she said.

'Steak and kidney pudding,' I said. 'But there isn't an earthly.'

'And syrup roll,' said Melly.

'I knew that's what you'd say,' said Mummy beaming. 'And that's just what we're having. And I've got a wonderful idea for a new story, and I'm going to start it this afternoon, while you three go out and try Blue Shadow over the jumps.'

So I spent the afternoon practising the jumps in Ann's field, on Blue Shadow. She jumped perfectly, but disliked being with the other ponies, and I could tell I was going to have to hold her hard.

Ann said, 'You don't know how I envy you. I can't think of anything more terrific than to jump two ponies at Chatton Show.'

'It depends how terrifically one jumps,' I said gloomily. 'I'm beginning to have the needle simply frightfully.'

Ann gave a scornful hoot. But I wished with all my heart that this had never happened, and that I was going to have the thrill – alas, now lost – of riding my darling Black Boy in his own little well-rehearsed show. That evening I was glad to find him much more comfortable, and I told him everything that had happened. Rapide was interested too.

'You've got to jump the best round you ever jumped in your life,' I told Rapide. 'Because though I want to win on Blue Shadow I don't want to see *you* beaten by *her*, and as I'm riding you both it doesn't make sense, does it?'

Rapide made one of his worst faces at me, which showed that he understood exactly what I was trying to say.

16
The great day

THE great days of one's life are supposed to dawn bright and clear; they always do in Mummy's books, where it says, 'The sun was shining and the birds were singing when Little Petronella awoke on what was to be her Great Day.' Alas, life is so little like books, and I can only say that dawn broke on the day of Chatton Show with a horrid drizzle, and I thought of the smell of wet macs, and wet horses and wet grass and wet spectators, and a lot of thoroughly wet disappointments. However, if any sensitive readers are by now in tears, I will reassure them by saying that by eleven o'clock in the morning it had cleared up, and though it was rather grey it was quite warm and I hastily checked over my outfit of clean jodhpurs, clean white shirt, well-pressed tie and well-polished boots. I brushed my jacket madly, and eventually discovered my hard hat under a lot of old newspapers in the Glory Hole under the stairs.

The pony classes did not begin until afternoon, so I had plenty of time to groom Rapide, though I have never known my fingers so thumb-like. When he was finished he looked like a polished chestnut, and I carefully packed up the grooming tools to give him another go-over before he entered the ring.

Mummy came out to watch me, and said, 'I've brought Black Boy an extra apple in case he feels sad at watching Rapide being got ready when he isn't.'

'He doesn't really seem to care much,' I said. 'He looks quite smug. He's been so spoilt the last day or two that he'll be unmanageable when he's better.'

'Lunch is at eleven-thirty,' said Mummy. 'It's better to have the spare time at the other end.'

'I shan't be able to eat a thing,' I moaned.

'Don't be silly,' said Mummy crisply, which I must confess did me a lot of good.

Then Melly and Lindo arrived with Blue Shadow who had been groomed by Pansy at Mrs Darcy's, and looked superb and very blue-ish. Her mane was beautifully plaited as only Pansy could do it, and her tail was like a fountain of silver light. Melly and Lindo were got up in their cream breeches, black coats, and riding boots that nearly blinded you, they were so bright.

'We're nearly dying with fright,' said Melly.

'Speak for yourself,' said Lindo. 'I'm not dying, I'm going to have a gorgeous time. Don't be such a wet, Melly. We've nothing to lose, and we might win something, and anyway, the only thing that matters is that Jill should do well.'

At hearing this noble sentiment fall from the lips of Lindo I nearly passed out cold.

'Lunch!' shouted Mummy from the back door.

'Oh, I couldn't eat a thing,' moaned Melly.

'Don't be silly,' said Mummy, and I giggled because it was exactly what she had said to me. We went in deciding we couldn't eat a thing, and packed away cutlets and cauliflower and roast potatoes and apple tart, which just shows you never know what you can do until you try; but I kept jumping up and down to see if I'd forgotten anything.

At last we were all ready to leave. Mummy was following on with some friends in their car.

'Good luck!' she said, waving us off. 'Ride slowly.'

Lindo rode Blue Shadow, I rode Rapide, and Melly rode the bike.

It wasn't very far to go, and everywhere there were yellow A.A. signs saying, To the Show.

'I expect all the other competitors will be terribly good,' said Lindo, sounding nervous for the first time.

'Oh, don't worry about them,' I said. 'Anyway, it's far better for you to feel the other competitors will be marvellous than to under-rate them. That's what usually lets you down.'

'Don't talk about being let down,' said Melly. 'I'm nearly falling off the bike with fright, so I'm sure to fall off the pony.'

We turned into Show grounds where already the stands were full, and crowds of people stood round the rails.

'There's half an hour before your class goes in, Lindo,' I said. 'We'll tie Rapide up, and then give Blue Shadow a last going over.'

When Lindo was ready I went and joined the crowd at the rails to watch. The first class came riding in, and there was Lindo, sitting very straight, a little too stiff, but terribly careful. Blue Shadow looked wonderful and walked like a princess. There was certainly no showing off about Lindo today; she had improved very much, and as the class walked round and then trotted and cantered she seemed to ease up and, keeping clear of other people, looked straight between Blue Shadow's firm, clear ears.

She was very noticeable, and the judges were favourably impressed. Lindo was called in first, and I saw her turn pale when she heard her number called. After the line-up and inspection she was handed the red rosette. I clapped madly as she rode out with quite a dazed look on her face, patting Blue Shadow's neck.

That's a good beginning, I thought; and just then I heard two women talking next to me, as they looked at their programmes.

'That pony that won — Blue Shadow,' said one of them. 'I'm sure I've seen her before. She's quite striking, but I didn't recognize the girl.'

'Why of course,' said the other, 'it's the pony that used to belong to the Graham girl, and was sold. She's a brilliant jumper, but too temperamental for words. Takes a dislike to another pony and simply dashes out of the ring.'

I felt as though I had been showered with cold water, but I tried to forget it, and went round to the exit to congratulate Lindo.

'Well, thank goodness that's over,' said Lindo, bursting with excitement. 'Now I can enjoy myself for the rest of the afternoon while you people suffer.'

'You were jolly good,' I said; and Mrs Darcy and Mummy came up to us and said, 'Well done, Lindo!'

'It wasn't me at all, it was Blue Shadow who did everything,' said Lindo, and again I was so surprised to hear such worthy sentiments flowing from her lips that I staggered. Lindo's character certainly was improving through contact with that noble creature, The Horse.

'Oh!' shrieked Melly. 'That's my class being called into the ring. Give me the pony! Oh, what shall I do?'

We all shouted things like 'Good luck!' and 'Keep calm,' and 'Ride easily' as Melly went in; but unfortunately, she did a lot of wrong things from sheer nervousness, as some people do, and I was sorry because she really could ride much better than the judges supposed. Still they must have been clever enough to realize this, because she got the reserve in the end, and was quite as pleased with it as Lindo had been with her first.

'I'm going to frame the certificate,' she said. 'I thought I should be right at the bottom of the unplaced line.'

I thought, Well, we've made a good beginning to Chatton Show, and now it's my turn; and at once I began to feel more frightened than I've ever felt in my life. We can't all do well, I thought, and this seems to be Lindo's day, and Melly's had some luck, too. Oh, Horrors! And then I remembered those two women by the rails discussing Blue Shadow, who had once belonged to a girl called Graham and had dashed out of the ring when she took a dislike to other ponies. I thought, Blue's the word! I felt slate-blue.

I expect you think I am an idiot to give way to such gloomy feelings, but you wait till something like that happens to you!

The weather was brightening by now, and the packed faces in the stands were suddenly flooded with sunshine. I couldn't help thinking what a gorgeous sight Chatton Show was, set in the huge parkland and surrounded with tall trees; the ring, and the white rails and the tall stands full of gay people, and the band in red coats and the marquees and flags; and crowds of people of all ages in riding clothes, and above all the horses – lovely, lovely horses being led up and down, or standing with flick of tail and jingle of bit under the trees. Somehow this magnificent sight gave me confidence; other people came here to enjoy themselves and I was going to enjoy myself too. After all, I was jolly lucky to be a rider and have a pony – two ponies! – to ride. What would I have felt like if I had been a poor little dressed-up kid sitting on the stand, just watching and envying and never having a chance? I went over and had a look at Rapide who was as calm as could be under his rug.

Mummy was there, and said, 'He's enjoying himself. He adores Shows.'

'So am I,' I said confidently. 'And I adore Shows, too.'

'Brace yourself up with an ice-cream,' said Mummy, 'and bring me one.'

I was very interested in the next event, which was the showing class with individual display, the one I should have entered with Black Boy. This was announced over the loud speakers as a Skill and Control competition for ponies of fourteen-two and under, and about twenty people lined up at the entrance to the ring, among them to my surprise my friend Ann Derry.

'Gosh!' I said. 'I didn't know you were in this. You're not down on the programme.'

'No,' she said, with a modest blush. 'I've been practising, but I didn't decide until yesterday that I was good enough to enter. And now I nearly wish I hadn't. All these others seem so frightfully competent.'

'What are you going to do?' I said.

Ann said I could jolly well wait and see. I thought she looked very neat and correct, and George was a pretty pony with loads of sense. He always carried his head and tail high, and today he wore some very nifty grey bandages over his white socks, and somehow matched well with Ann's dark-blue coat and blonde hair.

I soon saw that the trouble with most of the competitors was that they were trying to be too clever and ride full passes, pirouettes, and serpentines which they couldn't quite manage; and the ponies being too tensed up were snorting and prancing, and the judges were beginning to look a bit fed up at all these inexperienced people who thought they could do dressage, and obviously couldn't.

When it was Ann's turn she simply did the most perfect, slow, collected walk and trot I have ever seen – it looked easy but only those who understood realized the skill behind it – and then a few half passes, and then a perfectly-shaped figure of eight at the canter, three times, with a change of legs in the middle.

There was an absolute storm of clapping from all the know-how horsy people on the rails, and a man next to me said, 'Now that's what I like to see. A show that's simple and hundred per cent perfect. That fair kid has got everything. Look at her balance! She and that pony are a team.'

I couldn't help chipping in with, 'She's my greatest friend.'

'Well, she's good,' said the man. 'As for all those others who fancy they can change legs in the air, and only change the front legs and come down with the hind legs in a knot – give me strength!'

The clapping went on and on as Ann rode out, and I ran to meet her. She looked quite pale, as if she couldn't realize what all the applause was about.

'You were terrific,' I said. 'Everybody round me was saying so.'

'Well, thank goodness it came off,' said Ann. 'George was angelic.'

Soon the judges began to call in the winning numbers, 41, 27, 62, and 39.

'It's you!' I shrieked. 'Ann! *You're* 41.'

'It can't be,' said my dazed friend. I had to turn George for her and give him a push. Then Ann rode into the ring, and everybody began clapping again, and the judge handed her a red rosette. Was I pleased for her!

'I call that horsemanship,' said Mrs Darcy coming up behind me. 'Most of the others did fancy tricks, and didn't do them well. I'm proud of Ann.'

'Golly!' I said. 'So am I; and I'm proud of Lindo for winning the showing class, and Melly got a reserve which wasn't bad for *her* – but what about me?' And I began to tell her about the woman at the rails who had known Blue Shadow before, and how she didn't like jumping in front of other ponies.

'Look!' said Mrs Darcy, standing astride in her beautiful shining boots. 'Blue Shadow isn't a slug. She isn't a perfect jumping machine either. If she were I'd be insulting a girl like you in letting you ride her. She's full of temperament, and she needs the gentle and skilful handling of somebody who knows what's in her mind, and understands. You know what's in her mind – she doesn't like jumping in front of other ponies. Right! I believe you're a good and sympathetic enough rider to cope with her, and take her through. If I didn't I wouldn't let you ride her at all. I believe you've got her confidence, and if you feel her getting tense you'll know just what to do. And that's quite enough, Jill. So kindly stop beefing.'

After this I felt all topped up and yet humble, which I think is the right sensation and frame of mind for anybody entering a jumping competition.

There was an interval next while the jumps were erected; because they were having all the juvenile events in the first half of the programme, and the Grade C jumping and open jumping after tea.

My ponies were absolutely ready when it was time for me to lead them round to show them the jumps. It felt strange to me to be leading two, and I nearly jumped out of my skin when the loud-speakers suddenly announced, 'There is a correction in the entries for Class Four. Riding fifth should read, "Blue Shadow, owned by Miss Cortman, ridden by Jill Crewe." That is all.'

Gosh! I thought. And it's enough, too!

The jumps in the junior class were a brush, a gate, a stile, a wall, parallel bars, and finally a triple with quite a big spread. Walking round, they all looked enormous to me, but Rapide looked slightly bored and Blue Shadow only faintly interested.

I knew most of the people who were entering, and had ridden with them for years, so that made me feel more at home as we all waited outside the ring for the first number to be called in. That was Val Heath, an old friend of mine, and the one from whom I had most to fear, because she was an exceptionally good rider and hadn't any nerves. She pushed her hat back as she rode in and took the little practice jump.

'Bad sign,' said Ann, at my elbow. 'Val always does that when she isn't feeling so good.'

'Bosh!' I said. 'Look at her now.'

Val used her legs at the brush fence and took it with inches to spare; likewise the gate and the stile; then she turned her pony for the wall and jumped it too slowly amid a clatter of bricks.

'Four faults,' said Ann. 'If Val gets four she always gets eight. She can't stand anything but a clear round. Oh, look! She's lost a stirrup – and down goes the second bar!'

'Bad luck, Val,' we said as she rode out, and Val said, 'I always was a bad loser.'

When Ann rode in I found myself really wanting her to do well. George jumped as neatly as he always did, but he came to grief on the parallel bars and the triple, and somebody near me said, 'That triple's very tricky and the spread seems just too wide. It takes more than most of these kids have got to give.'

I remembered that as I heard my number called and rode in on Blue Shadow. I felt her tenseness, and whispered to her and held her tightly with my knees, trying to tell her how much I wanted from her. As we approached the brush I had one awful moment when I felt her falter as though for a refusal. These things take one second to happen and feel like an hour. Then the lovely pony gathered herself up and we sailed over like a bird. The gate and the stile were easy; at the wall I was certain I heard a click, but from the clapping I knew we were safely over. The parallel bars I took very cautiously, but Blue Shadow's own timing was perfect and I hardly had to help her. The triple! I thought. More than these kids know how to give? I'll show them!

I kept my fingers light and yet firm; I tried to breathe into Blue Shadow just what I wanted from her. I squeezed my knees against her ever so gently and held her, and held her, waiting for the exact split second, giving her time to collect herself. Then it came, the long spread in front of us, and I closed my eyes and sat low and let her go.

We were over! A clear round. I think my eyes were still shut as we trotted to the exit, and I patted and patted the smooth damp neck. I didn't care what happened next; I couldn't think beyond that clear round.

As I slipped down off Blue Shadow somebody thumped my back so hard that I nearly swallowed my tie, a few voices said, 'Nice work!' and my *bête noir* Susan Pyke, who was waiting in what looked like full hunting kit for the next class, said, 'Who on earth lent *you* that lovely pony? A baby could do a clear round on her.'

My one thought was, if only Rapide can do a clear round! I can't bear him to be beaten by Blue Shadow.

There were six people to ride before I went in again. I went to find Rapide who was having a confidential chat with Mummy. My dear, funny-looking, compact little show-jumper was as neat as a whistle and seemed alert and happy. He adored jumping and knew his turn would soon be coming.

Mummy said, 'You looked to be enjoying yourself on Blue Shadow.'

'I'm glad to hear that,' I said, 'because I was very worked up; the spread of that triple is really too much, but Blue Shadow was quite equal to it when she realized what I wanted.'

'And to me it looked easy,' said Lindo. 'It just shows. Gosh, I'm glad I didn't ride, I'd have come an awful cropper.'

'How is Rapide going to like it?' said Melly.

I made a face at Rapide who made a perfectly hideous one back at me, faces being his strong point.

'Rapide's unpredictable,' I said. 'There's nothing he can't jump if he wants to, but he's so theatrical, sometimes he thinks he's the Dying Swan.'

When my number was called I rode in. Rapide walked right round the practice jump as much as to say, 'What's that thing for?' I thought, 'Murder! He's going to be silly.'

But he wasn't, it was just that he didn't believe in wasting time on things that didn't count. He teetered up to the brush and hopped over it idly. Rapide, as I have told you in my previous books, has the weirdest action. He titt-ups along to his jump, stops practically dead, then bucks himself up in the middle and pops over. It makes people laugh until they realize that it is just Rapide's individual style, and very effective.

I was certain that he touched the stile, but it didn't come down. I sensed he was in the mood to 'do it all himself,' and I let him. Usually he disliked parallel bars, but this time he flicked over them as though they were nothing, and we approached the triple.

It's no good worrying about it, I thought. I'll give him the right aids and he'll have to do his best, and if he can't — well, he can't.

I tightened my fingers and pressed him and told him in our silent language that this one was a brute and he'd have to give it that much extra. Rapide knew. When he almost came to a standstill I thought, it's impossible! But I ought to have known Rapide. We sailed into the air; even then I thought we couldn't clear the third bar, but the next minute we were down and the clapping burst out all over the field.

I was delirious with happiness. A clear round for Rapide! I rode out and gave him a lump of sugar. I didn't care about anything now, not even the impending jump-off.

There were two other clear rounds. One was a farmer's daughter called Marion Dodsley whose pony could jump practically anything, because she hunted three days a week in the winter and went full tilt for stone walls, small rivers, and everything that came in her way. The other was John Hall, whom I knew very well, and as we waited he told me his clear round had been sheer luck and could never happen twice.

They gave us three jumps to do again. John Hall went first, and I think he was in a defeatist kind of mood because he brought something down at all three, and got eight faults. Then I went in on Blue Shadow and she took the whole thing in her stride; another clear round. Marion Dodsley also whisked over everything, rather contemptuously. I changed over to Rapide, and as we took the wall I heard the click of a dislodged brick. Two faults.

The judges asked if Marion and I would be willing to share the first prize and we agreed. So Blue Shadow got a red rosette, and Rapide third place and a yellow one. I was terribly happy.

'It's your day, isn't it?' said Mrs Darcy as I rode out.

'I don't know,' I said. 'I'll be up against some real competition in the senior class.'

We all went and had a nice long breather while they raised the jumps. Blue Shadow and Rapide each got a handful of oats, and looked quite beautifully smug wearing their rosettes, for now Blue Shadow had *two* red ones.

I swallowed several ice-creams in rapid succession. I thought, if I could choose who I'd be I wouldn't want to be anybody else. I felt very sorry for people who merely played tennis and ice-skated and went to ballet classes. I thought the Show ring was the jolliest place in the world, and horsy people the nicest people.

17
Well done, Rapide

WE were sitting on our ponies waiting to go into the ring for the senior jumping class. Everybody round me seemed to be much older and more experienced than I was, though I was fourteen and a half and nobody else was over sixteen, but you know how it is!

The judges walked into the ring looking very tweedy, except for one who wore a blue suit and a bowler hat, and carrying their shooting sticks to sit on. Judges usually do this, but hardly ever sit. It is just a habit.

'Don't the jumps look mountainous?' said a girl next to me whom I didn't know. I was surprised to hear her, because I had just been thinking gloomily how frightfully good she looked on her brown blood pony, with her dark-blue coat and spotless breeches and crash cap.

'I know,' she went on, 'that I'm going to muck everything up in the most ghastly way.'

I said, 'I suppose you're just saying that to appease Fate, because you always do a clear round,' and she said, 'I've never done a clear round in my life except in the paddock at home.'

I could hardly believe this, because she looked so smart and elegant, and as she rode in and cantered round to the first jump I wished I could look half as good as she did. She took the first three jumps beautifully, but at the fourth, for one of those unknown reasons ponies keep to themselves, she got three refusals and left the ring.

A boy behind me, with a checked cap rammed down over his eyes, said, 'I bet nobody does a clear round. They've put the jumps the wrong distances apart on purpose, to throw us off balance.'

I said, 'They couldn't do that under B.S.J.A. rules,' and he said, 'Oh, shut up, you don't know anything.'

I thought if he was in that sort of mood he wouldn't get very far round the course, and such was the case. He brought down the first three jumps, used his stick too much, and was ordered off by the judge. I thought it served him right, and I was sorry for his pony and hoped he would give up riding for ever.

'Number 61 disqualified,' shouted the loudspeaker. 'Number 29 now coming into the ring.'

'It's you,' said Melly, who with Lindo was anxiously hanging over me. 'I'm certain Blue Shadow will do it again.'

'Yum, yum!' said Lindo. 'It's an absolute cinch. Jolly good luck!'

I rode in with a good deal of confidence. I had tested Blue Shadow's quality already, and knew her style. She always approached the jump with her ears laid back; three paces away they came forward, her stride lengthened, and taking off at the right moment she sailed over. She was a very consistent pony when jumping.

Or so I thought. We cantered to the bottom of the ring and I brought her round to the first jump at a fair pace. She cleared the heightened brush easily, even scornfully, as much as to say, 'I like this paddock very much.'

Yes, paddock! For I fully believe that up to that moment Blue Shadow had been living in a kind of pleasant trance. And now the frightful thing happened. She realized in one fell swoop that she wasn't in a paddock at all! She was in a Show ring, jumping, with scores of other ponies and horses looking on.

Approaching the gate she suddenly pulled up and stood still with her forefeet planted, so that I just saved myself from going over her head. As I recovered my balance I could almost *hear* the silence of excitement all round me. I squeezed my knees gently and tightened my fingers on the single curb rein. But if the crowd were wanting wild west thrills they certainly got them. Blue Shadow gave a loud snort and broke into a frenzied gallop, faster and faster. I couldn't do a thing except stay on. Right round the perimeter of the ring she flew; and believe me, I have never ridden at such speed, and my thought was, Now I know what it feels like to win the Derby. We were making for the exit and the ponies waiting there were scattering in all directions. Through the empty space we galloped, and away towards the shelter of the trees. There at last I was able to slide down and bring the pony to a standstill. I could still hear the shrieks of laughter, consternation, and excitement coming from the crowd, and above all else the loudspeaker calmly proclaiming, 'Number 29 disqualified, number 46 now coming into the ring.'

Well! There it was! Blue Shadow had reverted to type, just like the women I had overheard had said, and I knew jolly well why the Graham girl had sold her.

Mrs Darcy, Melly and Lindo, Mummy and Ann were all rushing towards me.

'Are you all right, Jill?' said Mrs Darcy. 'You seemed to manage very well, considering. I never expected such a fiasco.'

'Manage!' I said with a hollow laugh. 'I just sat glued on.'

Lindo said, 'Good gracious! What made her bolt?'

I told her what I had overheard. 'She's a bolter,' I said. 'I ought to have been more careful, but I thought I was clever enough, and I wasn't.'

Melly burst out laughing. 'Oh, you did look funny!'

'Well, thank goodness *you* weren't on her,' I said. 'You'd have been mashed potato by now!'

Mummy said, 'You're supposed to be on again in half an hour, on Rapide. Are you all right? Or do you think you ought to scratch?'

'Scatch!' I said in horror. 'Gosh, no. I'll never feel right now until I've tried a round on a pony I can rely on. *And* I've learnt a few lessons. I was over-confident just now, and think if I'd been more careful I could have controlled Blue Shadow.'

I began to tidy myself up and Mummy brushed the back of my coat. Ann went back to the rails to see what was happening while Lindo brought me a lemonade, and came back to report, 'There've been two clear rounds. One of them is Susan Pyke.'

'Golly,' I groaned. 'This is going to be the end of everything. To be beaten by Susan Pyke! What a day!'

Mrs Darcy fetched Rapide. He looked sweet, and gleamed like a chestnut just out of the shell. 'Come on, boy,' I said. 'It's you and me for it. At least, I know that *you'll* never let me down, so anything that happens now will be my fault.'

'Attagirl!' said Mrs Darcy; and Mummy said, 'Don't try too hard, Jill. Remember that you're a junior jumping with seniors, and nobody expects much of you.'

'I expect a jolly lot of myself,' I said darkly, as I mounted and rode to the entrance, amid cries of 'Good luck.'

When I was called in there was quite a storm of applause, which cheered me up a lot. I don't know why there should have been; I suppose some people thought I would funk my second round. But the fact that I was surrounded by a sea of curious faces, hundreds of faces all staring at me, instead of terrifying me seemed to brace me up and give me just what I needed.

I'll show them! I thought.

I squeezed Rapide to a trot and we moved smoothly to the bottom of the ring; in front of me the brush fence looked not too frightening. I tickled Rapide's neck, he broke into a canter. Now he was off; he knew just when to make his peculiar little hesitation, then came the catlike jump. He flowed over the brush. Next came the narrow stile, and again I let him have it his way and again he was over. People were clapping now, and there before me reared the wall, dark and formidable and just that bit too high for my liking. 'Rapide can jump anything – anything, if he wants to,' I told myself, because it was true; and to prove me right he went over the wall like a lark. He wasn't pulling faces today, or acting up, or pretending; he was just jumping because he loved to and felt on top of the world.

I gave him a quick pat as we turned the corner and came up to the rather sticky in-and-out. This jump had been popped in to make things more difficult for some horses; but I was delighted, because it was Rapide's speciality. With his peculiar action he was able to do a beautiful rocking-horse movement, and taking just the right number of steps in between, do it again. We went well over the in-and-out; and now it was the parallel bars.

For the first time I felt a ripple of apprehension, or perhaps just tenseness, run through Rapide, and I knew I had got to feel sure of myself and convey that feeling to him. Come on, boy! I whispered. You mustn't, you mustn't refuse. Then I kicked. Up went his ears sharply, and the wings of the jump loomed up on either side, and up and over we went.

Only one more jump, the triple with its three spreading bars. He mustn't fear it, I thought, he must just treat it as nothing, it's the only way.

Steady, steady! I breathed, collecting Rapide as the jump came dead in front of us. He seemed to give a light-hearted little skip; the next minute we seemed to be right on top of the bars, hung in mid-air; I shut my eyes. We were over! I couldn't believe it when we lightly came to ground and cantered away.

A clear round! I patted Rapide with a trembling hand. 'You clever, clever, clever boy!' I said, and could hardly wait to get out of the ring before I gave him his handful of oats.

All my friends came round to congratulate me. I could only say, 'Rapide was wonderful. I don't care about anything now, I've done a clear round in the senior class.'

'You'll have to jump off again,' said Mummy, 'like you did in the junior.'

'I expect there'll be about ten clear rounds,' I said; but I was wrong. There were only three! – mine, and Susan Pyke's, and that of a girl called May Crawford who didn't come from our district. So Rapide was certain to get a prize, if it was only the third, which was far, far more than I had ever dared to hope for.

There were to be three jumps only for the jump-off. The judges decided quickly on the wall and the triple, and then hesitated for ages between the parallel bars and the in-and-out. I dug my fingers into my knees, knowing this meant my doom or the reverse. When they finally decided to retain the in-and-out I couldn't hold in my whoop of joy.

'What's up?' said Mummy.

'They've kept the in-and-out, and Rapide adores it!'

We three were called on the loud-speakers, and I went and joined Susan and the Crawford girl. The Crawford girl was rather nice, and said, 'My clear round was a fluke, I haven't an earthly. But you did so well before I'm sure you'll win.'

'Jolly good luck!' I said to her as she rode in; but I think her clear round must really have been a fluke, because she got two faults at each of the three jumps, and rode out with a rueful grin.

'They've widened the spread between the triple bars, that's the worst snag,' said Ann, as she and I stood watching Susan Pyke expertly dealing with the wall.

Susan approached the in-and-out and didn't seem too happy, but after one breathless moment when it looked as though her pony, Marquita, was going to refuse the second fence, all turned out well and she was safely over. But the tense moment had made Marquita excited, and she was fighting for her head as they came up to the extended triple. Susan cantered her slowly and showed some excellent horsemanship; then increased speed, but it was a fraction of a second too late. There was a click, and the second bar of the triple fell to the ground.

The crowds gave a groan. The loudspeaker said, 'Four faults.'

Susan rode out and I rode in. My fear was that Rapide would be a bit too confident, and he certainly took the wall too fast, but we were over it. My eyes were fixed on the in-and-out, but Rapide's little quiver of joy pleased me, for he was telling me clearly, Here's this nice jump again! I'll show them! He did his famous and funny cat jump, twice, and the crowd laughed and clapped as we cleared both sides of the jump with inches to spare.

I took him up to the triple carefully, for I knew it was too wide for him and my one hope was that I should get two faults for Susan's four. Instead of squeezing him I gave him two little kicks and he flew into the air. I heard something go down, and daren't think what it was. We were safe on the other side and cantering over the turf.

'Two faults,' said the loudspeaker. I could have yelled for joy. Wonderful, wonderful Rapide! I didn't know whether I was laughing or crying. I had won the senior jumping!

I rode out and joined Susan and May Crawford, and we all rode in again and got our rosettes, and back to our cheering friends. The scarlet gleamed above the yellow on Rapide's browband.

Mrs Darcy was holding out my black coat. 'Come on, you,' she said. I said, 'What's that for?' and she said, 'To go and get the Russell Cup, you goon!'

My mouth well open; I felt quite dithery. I hadn't even thought about the Cup. Somebody buttoned me into my black coat, and brushed my hat and put it on me, and even helped me up on Rapide. I rode into the ring and Colonel Russell handed me a large gleaming Cup, and I clasped it in my arms, and remembered to say, 'Thank you very much,' and he said, 'You've got a fine pony there,' and I said, 'Yes, I have'; and then I rode out again, nearly kicking myself for not thinking of something really intelligent to say, because I was sure Colonel Russell must think me a half-wit. I decided that the one sort of person I wanted to be was the sort of person who always thought of the right thing to say at the right time, and not next morning.

18
They're going!

I HAD won eleven pounds in prize money, and as five of them had been won by Blue Shadow in the junior jumping I felt that Melly and Lindo ought to have that amount. But they wouldn't take it.

'You did all the work,' said Melly, 'so you're jolly well going to have the prize.'

'But she was your pony,' I pointed out.

'Well, she isn't our pony now,' said Lindo. 'I think it was awfully decent of Mr Prescott to say he'd take her, and see if he could cure her of her fault.'

'And if he can't,' said Melly, 'he'll loan her to the riding school, because she's marvellous *except* in the show ring, in spite of being called a show jumper.'

'And I'll tell you something else,' said Lindo. 'Melly and I have decided we've had enough of ponies. We're not cut out for the world of equitation and we're going back to dogs.'

Which on the whole, I think, was as well. I was delighted to have eleven pounds for my ponies' winter fodder and stable expenses; and Black Boy's injury was nearly cured, and everything was lovely. We were out in the orchard now, offering Black Boy a carrot or two; he had become very spoiled by the petting he had got during his lameness, and I could see I was going to have to be very tough with him soon.

'I simply can't realize,' said Melly, 'that we're going home tomorrow. I never knew anything go so quickly.'

Yes, the Cortmans' visit had really come to an end, and I was glad Melly thought it had gone quickly. To me it felt like one hundred years.

'We've ordered you a farewell present to remember us by,' said Lindo. 'Mummy told us to.'

'Oh, thank you very much,' I said politely, wishing I could have been asked what I wanted, and dreading one dozen linen handkerchiefs in a dainty case, or perhaps the wrong sort of gloves.

'I've got to tell you what it is,' burst out Melly. 'I can't hold it in, so stop glaring at me, Lindo. It's a new saddle for Black Boy.'

I nearly fell over backwards. I could only gulp. How I had misjudged these girls! 'Oh, how wonderful!' I gasped. 'How absolutely smashing! I say!'

'Well, we did him in,' said Lindo, 'so we felt we owed him something, and I hope he'll win millions of rosettes when he's wearing his new saddle.'

'It *is* decent of you,' I gulped. 'Thank you fifty million times. You make me feel rather a beast.'

'Oh, shucks,' said Melly. 'We're rather beasts ourselves at times. Everybody is.'

So the next morning came, and Mummy and I stood on the station platform seeing Melly and Lindo off, while they hung out of the carriage window, and the guard packed the struggling dogs away in his van.

'Do write,' said Melly, 'and tell us if Black Boy likes his saddle.'

'We'll write to you,' said Lindo, 'and tell you about school, which is all we'll have to tell you about. School! Help!'

'Good-bye! Good-bye! And jolly good luck!' Mummy and I yelled madly, as the train began to pull out. We went on waving until it was out of sight.

Mummy went on into Chatton to do some shopping, and I strolled off alone. It was a lovely day and the sun was sparkling on the hedges of the country lanes. I would go home and take Rapide for a canter over the Common where the gold gorse bushes were gleaming under the blue sky. I began to run and as I ran I whistled, which is quite difficult to do. You have to be feeling very happy. The Cortmans had gone. They had turned out to be so much more decent than I had expected, as people nearly always do, and we had had lots of adventures together; but it was lovely to be alone again.

I raced into the orchard and put one arm round Rapide's neck and one round Black Boy's and they nuzzled my shoulders. Just me and my ponies! Wonderful!

JILL'S GYMKHANA

RUBY FERGUSON

This is the FIRST of the 'Jill' books, the most popular and delightful pony stories of all.

Life is not easy for Jill's family, but she manages to buy a pony and sets about learning to ride. At the same time she has the task of making friends at her new school and earning money to pay for the pony's keep.

In spite of rebuffs and hardships, Jill is determined to succeed, particularly as the gymkhana gets nearer ...

KNIGHT BOOKS

If you enjoyed this book you may also like to read the other books by Ruby Ferguson in the 'Jill' series:

JILL ENJOYS HER PONIES
PONY JOBS FOR JILL
JILL AND THE PERFECT PONY
JILL'S PONY TREK
JILL'S GYMKHANA
A STABLE FOR JILL
JILL'S RIDING CLUB
JILL HAS TWO PONIES

KNIGHT BOOKS